Ki paused . . .

He could hear a shuffling in the underbrush ahead as the man swiveled to bring his revolver to bear. Ki scarcely had an instant's grace to dart aside before the revolver lanced flame and lead ricocheted off the rocks next to him in a shower of sparks.

Instantly, Ki lunged forward, slashing underhanded with his knife. The blade bit into the man's belly, and Ki sliced upward through his brisket as though gutting an animal. Warm blood gushed over the hilt and his hand. The man teetered away, off the blade, and spun over the edge in a long fall to the gorge below . . .

Also in the LONE STAR series from Jove

LONGARM AND THE LONE STAR LEGEND
LONE STAR ON THE TREACHERY TRAIL
LONGARM AND THE LONE STAR VENGEANCE
LONGARM AND THE LONE STAR BOUNTY
LONE STAR AND THE HANGROPE HERITAGE
LONE STAR AND THE MONTANA TROUBLES
LONE STAR AND THE MOUNTAIN MAN
LONE STAR AND THE STOCKYARD SHOWDOWN
LONE STAR AND THE RIVERBOAT GAMBLERS
LONE STAR AND THE MESCALERO OUTLAWS
LONE STAR AND THE AMARILLO RIFLES
LONE STAR AND THE SCHOOL FOR OUTLAWS
LONE STAR ON THE TREASURE RIVER
LONE STAR AND THE MOON TRAIL FEUD
LONE STAR AND THE GOLDEN MESA
LONGARM AND THE LONE STAR RESCUE
LONE STAR AND THE RIO GRANDE BANDITS
LONE STAR AND THE BUFFALO HUNTERS
LONE STAR AND THE BIGGEST GUN IN THE WEST
LONE STAR AND THE APACHE WARRIOR
LONE STAR AND THE GOLD MINE WAR
LONE STAR AND THE CALIFORNIA OIL WAR
LONE STAR AND THE ALASKAN GUNS
LONE STAR AND THE WHITE RIVER CURSE
LONGARM AND THE LONE STAR DELIVERANCE
LONE STAR AND THE TOMBSTONE GAMBLE
LONE STAR AND THE TIMBERLAND TERROR
LONE STAR IN THE CHEROKEE STRIP
LONE STAR AND THE OREGON RAIL SABOTAGE
LONE STAR AND THE MISSION WAR
LONE STAR AND THE GUNPOWDER CURE
LONGARM AND THE LONE STAR SHOWDOWN
LONE STAR AND THE LAND BARONS
LONE STAR AND THE GULF PIRATES
LONE STAR AND THE INDIAN REBELLION
LONE STAR AND THE NEVADA MUSTANGS
LONE STAR AND THE CON MAN'S RANSOM
LONE STAR AND THE STAGECOACH WAR
LONGARM AND THE LONE STAR MISSION
LONE STAR AND THE TWO GUN KID
LONE STAR AND THE SIERRA SWINDLERS
LONE STAR IN THE BIG HORN MOUNTAINS
LONE STAR AND THE DEATH TRAIN

WESLEY ELLIS

LONE STAR

AND THE RUSTLER'S AMBUSH

A JOVE BOOK

LONE STAR AND THE RUSTLER'S AMBUSH

A Jove Book/published by arrangement with
the author

PRINTING HISTORY
Jove edition/June 1987

ISBN: 0-515-09008-5

Jove Books are published by the Berkley Publishing Group,
200 Madison Avenue, New York, NY 10016. The words
"A JOVE BOOK" and the "J" with sunburst are trademarks
belonging to Jove Publications, Inc.

PRINTED IN THE UNITED STATES OF AMERICA

Chapter 1

Through the rainstorm of the late-summer afternoon, the Chicago & North Western train chugged westward across the timbered slopes and rocky flats of central Wyoming Territory. Since Casper, some time before, the train had been flanking the Badwater River, easing around gullies and toiling up brushy grades, dawdling at every riverbank hamlet like the branchline local it was. Along about Shoshone, though, the train curved southerly and soon was paralleling the Wind River, crossing from one bank to the other and then back again as it wound among jagged outcrops and massed boulders.

As swiftly as the rain began, it tapered to a drizzle and then ceased altogether, scudding north with growly thunderclouds and flashes of heat lightning. Sunset from a clearing sky burnished the C&NW's ten-car bobtail haul of flats, boxes, and coaches with slanting rays. The steam of evaporating rainwater made the purpling mountains and muddied expanses dance weirdly, when viewed through a coach's blown-glass windows.

"Riverton! Nex' stop!" an elderly conductor called, entering the coach where Jessica Starbuck and Ki were seated. "Gateway o' the Shoshone, er, now Wind River Indian Reservation. Stage connections to Fort Brown—I mean, Fort Washakie—an' for Morton, Crowheart, and points thataway." Muttering to himself, "Wish they'd quit changin' names—one's enough for any spot," the conductor lumbered on through to the next coach. "Ar-rivin' Riverton . . . !"

"High time," Ki groused as he rose and stretched his cramped legs. "By the schedule, we're getting in four hours late."

"And're getting off foul with dust, soot, and sweat," Jessie added wearily, stuffing the papers she'd been reviewing back in their manila folder. "Before any freshening up, though, we really should find Slats Burdou and hear the Box M's side, learn what it knows about this puzzling mess. That includes why he needed us to meet him in Riverton, way away from Box M's bailiwick around South Powder River. Hopefully Slats will be waiting at the Continental Hotel, like he wired last week, staying low till we could reach him."

"Hopefully your hope isn't misplaced," Ki responded wryly, taking his small Gladstone and Jessie's leather bellows bag down from the overhead rack. "We don't know Burdou, never met him or his boss Hep Mulhollan, but they don't shine too bright in light of the evidence."

"Maybe, but all the facts aren't in yet. And up to now, Mulhollan has managed the Box M for Starbuck efficiently and honestly, and he must've found Burdou trustworthy enough to've made him foreman. No, I still believe the Box M honored its contract, as they claim, and shipped a herd of prime beef to the army, instead of the low-grade soup cows that somehow arrived."

"If so, then obviously the Box M stock was substituted with cull stuff somewhere en route. But Mulhollan not only swears he supervised the loading at Natrona, but saw that the cars were sealed when the C and NW train left. The army authorities swear the cars were still sealed a day later, when the train was shunted onto the military sidetrack at Riverton. And Fort Washakie's head honcho, Major Thinnes himself, was on hand when the cars were unsealed at the fort and the culls unloaded. Now, they can't all be telling the truth."

"They can, if both the Box M and the army were

tricked by some very slick rustlers, a gang of switcheroo artists. It's a hunch, I admit, and as these reports and telegrams show—" Jessie tapped the file as she slid it into her bag—"everything points to a swindle by the supplier. The army can prove its case, I'm afraid, for voiding the contract, suing the Box M bankrupt, and jailing Mulhollan on a charge of defrauding the federal government."

"Great. We can't prove we even have a case," Ki responded, leading the way down the aisle, maneuvering the two bags with the swaying of the carriage. "If there is one, it's as much a mystery to the Box M bunch as it is to us."

The coach carried a large quota of gentry, but there were a number of fancy Dans and grubstake seekers, and quite a few troopers on leave. Or so Jessie and Ki estimated. In turn, the passengers surveyed them in passing.

Men admired Jessie as they watched her stride by. She had a walk both assured and lithe, almost masculine; yet there was never a woman more feminine, or more capable of arousing male lust. In her mid-twenties, she was heiress to the immense Starbuck business empire. The voluptuous curves of her breasts and thighs moved with sleek sensuality within her stylish two-piece outfit of summer-weight beige wool. Equally stylish was her turban hat, which hid the coils of her copper-blond tresses, but did little to conceal her cameo-shaped face. Pert-nosed and full-mouthed, she exuded an inner core of warmth and passion and courage. But at the moment, she also reflected her grave determination to meet and beat this latest threat. That was why she discreetly carried her custom .38 Colt pistol in her jacket, and a two-shot .38 derringer tucked in her dainty chatelaine purse. A lady could never be too careful.

Similarly, women cast intrigued glances at Ki. Born

of a Japanese woman wedded to an American, he was a handsome blend of both races—tall, bronze-complected, with blue-black straight hair, a strong-boned face, and almond eyes of a dark and vital intensity. Orphaned in Japan, he had emigrated to America, where he had been hired by Jessie's father, Alex Starbuck, to guard her from criminal harm. Such peril was real. As a babe, Jessie had lost her mother to lawless killers, and eventually her father too was murdered and subsequently avenged. Ki stayed on, her brotherly companion and confidant; now in his early thirties, he was ready as ever to protect Jessie and her far-flung interests.

As befitting his task, Ki wore a discreet brown traveling suit and, instead of boots, a pair of Asian rope-soled cloth slippers. He didn't pack a gun; nor did he use one as a rule. Yet he was anything but defenseless. Lethal power lay in his relaxed yet iron-hard body, for he was samurai-trained in the martial arts, an expert with the slim daggers and other weapons, including little star-shaped razored disks called *shuriken,* which were stashed in his clothes.

If he and Jessie noticed the stares, however, they gave no indication. They stepped out onto the platform and waited with four other passengers while the train, slowing, chuffed down the center of Riverton's main street. It was the usual rural town street: a widened strip of wagon road knifing between twin rows of false-fronted buildings, a few houses, and a large stockyard. During the dry season, its hardpan pavement would become a ribbon of dust hock-deep to a horse. In wet weather, the street and adjacent bare land would become a swamp—it was pretty well nigh to that now; the earth had been churned boggy by the recent rainstorm, and was pitted and slashed by hoofs, feet, and wagon wheels.

Bell clanging, smoke belching, the locomotive

lurched to a halt beside a small depot, which was flanked on both sides by loading chutes and holding pens. Descending from the train, Jessie and Ki started toward the near end of the pens, most of which were filled with bawling cattle. The cattle were fat after months of feeding on Wyoming grass. The best of them carried the LXD brand of the nationally renowned Ledditt & Dinsmore beef syndicate. At this same yard, Jessie reflected, an equally prime herd of Box M–supplied and U.S.–branded cattle had waited while the C&NW unhitched it, and the Army took over its transport to Fort Washakie, westward across the rugged reservation. At least, it had been assumed at the time that it was a trainload of plump, juicy cows.

Walking along the cinder apron, Jessie and Ki tried to avoid the mud as they scanned for the Continental Hotel. It was hard to see, dusk having fallen; and plenty of bystanders and travelers were milling about trackside. What with the hubbub, the mooing, and noises from the train, it also was difficult to hear particulars. It was already too late when Ki heard a soft hissing by his head and twisted around. The noose of a lasso rope sailed down over him, pinning his arms to his sides. The bags dropped and Jessie gasped in shock, as the rope tautened and, with a vicious jolt, yanked Ki off his feet.

Ki hit the mud in a sliding belly-flop. The rope rapidly pulled him, rolling and twisting, headlong through a gumbo of mud, rocks, and animal wastes. He was dragged almost a hundred yards before it ceased as quickly as it had begun, and he skidded to a halt. He lay there for a moment, catching his wits as well as his breath, before wrenching his body around.

He couldn't see Jessie yet, though he could hear her way behind, shouting angrily as she ran. He focused instead on the legs of three horses directly ahead, then gazed up at the men in the saddles. All wore ordinary range garb in sad need of washing, caked cowboots, and holstered revolvers. Two were snickering; they were strangers to Ki, with a certain hard-case stamp to them, he thought.

The third man, to whose saddle horn was tied the rope, struck Ki as vaguely familiar. Ruddy-haired and bearded, he had the height and brawn of an Irish bruiser combined with the leaner, darker features of a Latin—the not uncommon by-product of railroad laboring in the Southwest, but quite rare this far north. Some time past, his nose had been broken and had healed crookedly, giving the bridge an S curve and the bushy brows a perpetual scowl, shadowing his deep-socketed, obsidian-bright eyes. Recognition hit Ki then, in a flash of memory. "Oscar Pascal!"

"You din' forget me, eh?" Pascal grinned, exposing stumps of teeth. Ki himself had smashed them out five years ago, when the Circle Star had fought to capture Pascal and his outlaw pards for cattle rustling. Pascal had had a straight nose then, no gray hair, and had weighed forty pounds less. Prison had exacted its toll. "I sure din' forget you, Ki. T'was such a surprise to spot you climbin' off the train, how'msoever, I almost disbelieved you was you."

Ki struggled to his knees. "Get this rope off me, Pascal."

"Not afore I'm of a mind to. What brung you this far afield, anyhow?"

"I could ask you the same," Ki hedged.

"Implyin' the law should, an' I'm an escaped con, eh? Bull! Same's when I was set free down south, and nobody'd give me a break, just a lotta bull. Had to trek north for work, an' got a job running cattle purely legit an' respectable. I'm now foreman of the LXD spread o'er by the Bridger Mountains. And I owe you for all of it," Pascal sneered, curveting his horse backward, the abrupt jerk spilling Ki back down in the muck. "I owe you from that first time, an' for the time I served; an' I ne'er forgot nary a tick of it."

"I don't keep books," Ki growled as he awkwardly regained his knees. "You earned your due, paid your debt, and don't owe anybody anything."

"Yeah? Well, I'm doing the bookkeeping. You cost me long misery, an' I'm paying you back, with interest." Again he whirled his horse, and again Ki was hurled flat on his face, the rope drawing tight as Pascal readied to spur forward.

Then: "Stop where you are, or I'll stop you with lead!"

The rope suddenly slackened. Groping, slipping, Ki rose kneeling once more, wiped the goop from his eyes, and was relieved to see Jessie standing nearby. Infuriated, her expression and voice brooking no argument, she held her pistol centered implacably on Oscar Pascal. Also gratifying to Ki was the sight of Pascal caught flat-footed and flustered, making no move toward his staghorn-butted S&W .44's set high and handy in their cutaway holsters—though that didn't squelch Pascal from demanding gun action from his two sidekicks.

"You've got irons! No female pistol-packer's any lady or any shootist!"

"That's what we're afraid of," one man replied. "She might go wavery and hit us by mistake, if she takes notion to fire point-blank at you, boss."

"Will you quit stalling'? F'Gawd's sake, pull your drop on her!"

"Pull, and you'll push grass," Jessie warned. "Pascal goes first."

Pascal's mouth clamped and his eyes were ebon fire. "By hell, you Starbucks ain't satisfied with hogging half o' Texas, you gotta horn in here like you own Wyoming, too. Like just 'cause you're uppity rich, you reckon you got a right to blast anyone who don't jump when you holler frog—"

"Try me," she cut in, looking eager. "Or hop to, and untie that rope."

Pascal loosened the end snubbed to the horn, cursing luridly—and mainly at the men. "Yaller pissants! One bullet would've done it!"

"Maybe, but you'd be dead," Jessie responded grimly, turning a trifle to watch Ki free his arms and slip the noose off. "Are you all right?"

"Fine. I bet I'll feel even dandier real soon, too." Slowly, Ki walked toward Pascal. He reeled a little, and his vision still wasn't entirely clear. One thigh was sorely bruised from the sharp gouge of some buried stone. His suit was in tatters, yet it stuck to his body, held together by the slathers of mud, grit, fodder, and droppings that covered it. His face, too, smarted under a coat of stockyard sludge.

"With a big outfit like the LXD you could go far, assuming you'll keep the law and've flung your last crooked loop. That'd be the loop, Pascal, you threw to rope and then drag me," Ki noted as he approached, his manner icily calm, his eyes inscrutable. "Nobody can do what you tried to do to me and get away with it—nobody. And Pascal, I'm going to take you apart with my bare hands."

Leaping, Ki grabbed Pascal by the shirt. Pascal reared, blurting an oath, fumbling for a gun. His pals barked protests but sat still for it, continuing to respect Jessie's pistol more than Pascal's honor. Jessie chilled, knowing Ki was adept enough and fearing he was angry enough to kill Pascal easily. Ki was ready to maim Pascal; he was also aware that'd be an overly harsh and stupid reaction. His martial arts would look so wierd and exotic to the locals that it could draw too much attention and suspicion their way. Moreover, the pair siding with Pascal might get mad and do something foolish. Besides, what with one thing and another, Ki was feeling wringy enough to whump Pascal at his own sport, the down 'n' dirty gutter brawl.

Ducking a wild swing, Ki hauled Pascal loose of the saddle. Down 'n' dirty Pascal came, diving like a cannonball, and ramming full-bodied into Ki. The force knocked Ki backward off his feet, with Pascal falling atop him and flailing him with both fists. They rolled over and over in the mud, hammering at each other. A slanting blow to Pascal's left eyebrow drew blood. He jabbed a thumb at Ki's eyeball, only to take a knuckle in the throat that set him to gagging, his hands dropping. Immediately, Ki shoved free and launched to his feet.

Scrambling, Pascal rushed in with arms swinging like windmills. Ki dodged a high left, weaved in close and buried a stiff jab in Pascal's midriff. Pascal gasped and bent, still swinging, and received a split second left-right combo to both eyes. Then Pascal scored an uppercutting haymaker that crunched against Ki's jaw with meaty impact, sending him staggering off-balance. Ki shook his head to clear it, falling back a pace to regain his footing, as Pascal confidently charged to polish him off.

Ki evaded the storming fists, dancing aside and hammering at Pascal's gut and heart. The counter caught Pascal surprised and unguarded, and though he tried to slug back, Ki kept darting around and under, pummeling the belly and face, driving Pascal the length of the pen and pinning him against its fence.

Pascal rebounded, grappling, to wrap Ki in a crushing bearhug. Suspecting such a move, Ki was prepared for it and caught Pascal by the whiskers, jerking his face down, mashing the once-broken nose against his rising right knee. He felt the cartilage crush, saw the blood from the flattened nostrils as he pushed Pascal aside. Like a blundering, blind bull, Pascal shuffled and charged head down, groping, ignoring Ki's hits, battering through Ki's guard, and taking a jab on the top of the head that nearly cracked Ki's knuckles. Then Pascal got his arms around Ki, lifted him whirling, and heaved him away.

Ki struck the sodden earth with a bone-shaking splash. Bellowing, Pascal loped at Ki, blood trickling from his nose and mouth, one eye closed, and the other puffed and bruised. Yet a homicidal light burned from his injured face as his sharp-heeled boots canted toward Ki's chest. Desperately Ki wrenched aside, grasping Pascal's descending foot to avert the crippling stomp. But he was not quite fast enough. The boot tramped down upon his left shoulder. Hot lances of agony ripped through his bludgeoned sinews, while with his hand still clasped around the boot, he coiled his legs beneath Pascal's belly and thrust upward with all his strength. Retching, Pascal reeled back, toppling askew and falling flat on his face.

Ki pounced on Pascal before he could recover. Snatching a fistful of his shaggy hair, Ki pounded his head up and down with a wicked, rhythmical beat, grinding and drumming Pascal senseless. Then, wavering, Ki rose and glared down, panting, at Pascal lying half-submerged and unmoving in the mire.

"He's all yours," he said, as he dragged Pascal by the collar toward the two glum-faced men. He cast a grin at Jessie, who pocketed her revolver, though she kept her hand in there with it, Ki observed. Then he saw, beyond her and the clump of gawkers, a great, solid fellow approaching, a five-pointed star pinned to the lapel of his black clawhammer coat. The coat hung open and exposed a cartridge belt and long-barreled Colt, and a shotgun nestled in the crook of his arm.

"Hold it, you!" he shouted at Ki over the crowd.

"Quinby," one of Pascal's companions noted, flat and expressionless. The other nodded.

"You take him from here, back to where he belongs," Ki told them, and let go of Pascal, who sunk unconscious to the ground. "I figure we're even."

The lawman barged through and stopped, gazing at Pascal, then frowning at Ki. "Big mistake, committin' assault and battery. What's your name?"

"Ki. I didn't attack, either. I was ending it."

"Your full name, first an' last."

"Just Ki, Marshal."

"District Sheriff Quinby to you, Jess Ki," he said, misunderstanding. He was dishwater-blond, bigger than Ki or Pascal, with a thick neck and a heavy jaw. He sported mutton chops, had a direct look to his blue eyes, and in sum seemed a fairly handsome, decent sort. Yet, sizing him up, Ki didn't like the shape of his mouth. The lips were too thin and the mouth was turned down at the corners. "Don't appear self-defense to me, but p'raps it will to the judge. Depends on the witnesses." Sardonically he eyed the two men. "You're with Pascal, right? You must've seen the fight begin, who started it. Well?"

To Ki's surprise, they refused the chance to lie him into jail, perhaps afraid it'd backfire later and land them and Pascal into real trouble. After exchanging glances, one said, "Tell you factually, Sheriff, from what we saw of it, everyone slipped bad in the mud. Maybe they'd had a drink too many."

The crowd hooted, laughing. Quinby grimaced, realizing he'd been done in, and exasperatedly gripped Ki by the arm. "Okay, for this time. They got their reasons, I reckon, but I got my notions. You best not settle here permanent."

"Only stopping over, Sheriff. Where's the Continental Hotel?"

"Halfway back on t'other side o' th' street. It's for gents."

"Maybe they'll make an exception for me," Ki replied wryly. Keeping relaxed, he went over to Jessie, retrieved their bags, and headed toward the hotel, Jessie strolling alongside. Just before the end of the stockyard, he felt the impulse to turn and glance back.

The crowd was thinning, discussing the choicer points of the fight as they went their ways. Pascal's sidekicks had dismounted and were carting him by his shoulders and legs, preparing to toss him over his saddle. Neither they nor anyone else was paying attention to Jessie or Ki. Nobody except Quinby, that is, who stood, legs akimbo, eyeing the two as if they were mere casual passersby. But the cradled shotgun with its barrel lying across his left forearm didn't look casual at all.

Chapter 2

"By the skin of your teeth," Jessie observed, as they angled in the direction of the hotel. "I was about to interfere when Pascal's buddies told that absurd story. Sheriff Quinby was sure out to jug you, legal or not."

"Well, he didn't know me, didn't know what'd gone on, but he'd know the LXD would have a powerful crew and influential bigwigs to back one of their own. Even if the one was a known rustler like Pascal." There was no sign of anger or resentment on Ki's face, except for the fact that one eye was squinting and his lips were drawn back from clenched teeth. "Jessie, he's the answer. Pascal's your explanation for Box M's missing beefs."

Jessie shook her head. "Tempting . . . and Pascal must've been hired without being checked, which can happen in big operations like the LXD," she said, aware that Ledditt & Dinsmore was a reputable yet large and unwieldy stock consortium. They had holdings in America, Canada, and the Argentine, and supplied the abattoirs of Europe with meat, wool, and hides. "But it's not as simple as that, Ki. Pascal may be going straight, for all we know. After all, he can't have been out of prison long enough to've rounded up much of a rustler gang. When I wire the Circle Star later on, though, I'll see what can be discovered about Pascal."

A C&NW work engine snorted over by the yards. Somewhere a blacksmith's sledge rang on an anvil. A half-dozen horses stood hipshot at the tie-rack fronting the hotel—a two-story plankboard building with a whitewashed false front. Above the crowded porch, where a wooden awning made a series of sway-backed scallops, rose a hand-lettered sign: CONTINENTAL HOTEL & CLUB.

"If this place is considered fit for gentlemen," Jessie remarked, shuddering slightly as they entered, "I'd hate to see Riverton's other holes."

Except for a small lobby with a desk and a staircase, the lower floor was given over to a barroom and gambling hall—the club portion of the Continental. Raucous noise filtered from its doorway, along with the fetid odors of tobacco smoke, cheap whiskey, cheaper perfume, and sweaty flesh.

A sleepy, rat-face clerk at the reception desk had a different aroma about him, that of *eau de rose*, and was obviously an insufferable prig. His beady eyes centered on Jessie, who was a few paces ahead of Ki, and he declared with a long-nosed sniff, "Room will be four dollars a night, in advance."

"Two, please, one for myself and one for my friend," Jessie replied, sliding two five-dollars pieces across the counter. "Which room is Mr. Burdou in?"

"Twenty-three." The clerk, pocketing the coins, glanced at the key board behind him. "But Mr. Burdou is out at the moment. Dinner, more'n likely, which he usually returns from in about an hour. Anything else?"

Ki spoke up. "Yeah, a bath. And do you have laundry service?"

"Bath is fifty cents extra, fresh water each morning, at the end of the upstairs hall. We've a maid who does washing and ironing as a sideline, and— Great Judas Priest!" The clerk recoiled, having finally taken a good look, not to mention a good whiff, of Ki. "The Continental does have certain minimum standards, mister. Who d'you think you are to come in so—so repulsive!"

"The tooth fairy, and yours are up for grabs," Ki

snapped, smearing muck on the register and counter as he made a lunge at the insulting clerk.

"Gah!" Paling, the clerk backed against the key rack, pawed frantically, and lobbed a key across at Ki. "Here! Take the room! Sign in later, whatever room it is, just don't touch me!"

Grinning, Ki and Jessie crossed to the stairs, where Jessie paused to tell the appalled clerk, "I think I'd like a bath, too. Clean and hot, of course. You'll see to it that the water is changed for me, won't you?"

"Changed! Ma'am," he replied frigidly, "after your friend is done polluting it, I'll see to it that the entire tub is carried out and buried."

They mounted the stairway, the sounds and smells of the barroom below fading as they turned left down a long, murky corridor flanked by closely spaced doors. Jessie stopped at room 15 and fitted her key in the lock.

"Maybe you'd better bathe now, Ki," she suggested, opening the door, "before the clerk reports you to Sheriff Quinby as a health hazard. I'll go see if I can get a lead on Slats Burdou, and meet you back here in an hour."

"If you're earlier, I'll be in the tub or my room, number seven."

Leaving Jessie her bellows bag, Ki went to his room. It was in keeping with the rest of the hotel, with a plain bureau, a drab armchair, and a large wardrobe sporting a full-length, discolored mirror. The bed was sway-backed with a dreary blue spread, but seemed to be relatively bug-free. Opening his Gladstone, he gathered clean clothes and wrapped them in a towel, and went out locking the door behind him, and headed down the hall to the bathroom.

The bathroom was not in use. The door hook seemed to latch okay, but just in case, Ki folded the towel so his straight-blade razor could be reached quickly from the zinc tub of tepid water. Cautiously satisfied, he slipped into the tub and, with a bar of yellow soap, scrubbed himself thoroughly. After a rinse, he eased lower until the water crept up to his chin and his knees emerged. He closed his eyes, enjoying the well-deserved soak.

"Ahhh," he sighed contentedly.

Suddenly a frown furrowed on Ki's forehead. A cool draft was tickling his knees. Without opening his eyes, he murmured drowsily, "I could swear I locked that door."

Someone giggled. "You did, but it doesn't hold that way."

Ki jerked upright in the tub, his hand darting for the razor as he gazed at a young woman standing inside the doorway. She was shutting the door behind her and locking it correctly. "I wasn't expecting any visitors," Ki said, self-consciously scratching his bare chest. "Especially a lady."

"Heavens, a girl doesn't work at a hotel without seeing men in all states of undress," she said, smiling reassuringly as she stepped closer. "Truth is, it's you who should be think improper of me, coming in without knocking."

"Why, such a notion never crossed my mind," Ki assured her with a straight face. "Is this social or are you the back-scrubber, ma'am?"

"Prudence," she corrected, sitting primly on the rolled tub-rim. She was ripe and pretty, in a loud way, with big silver earrings and sleek brown hair pulled back and set low on her neck in a bun. She wore a tight green dress that showed off her nubile figure so well that Ki wondered if she had anything on under it. There wasn't any reason to believe that was the only thing she was wearing, but somehow he got that idea. "Melvin down at the desk told me the bather in room seven needed some laundry burned, and that'd be you, wouldn't it? And aren't you the fellow who tuckered Oscar Pascal?"

Ki looked impressed. "Word moves quickly in Riverton, doesn't it?" Before the girl could respond, he leaned toward her, moving his hand from his razor, and whispered conspiratorially, "Pascal slipped."

"Oh, no, he's a notorious bully, overdue for a hiding. How wonderful! You had cause; I'm just sure he must've given you good reason. Didn't he?"

"You ask his buddies," Ki replied, wondering what she was waltzing up to. "Ask the sheriff, even, if Pascal wasn't maybe tipsy and slipped."

"You're simply being modest." She bent nearer, intimacy creeping into her voice. "You got what-for against him, don't you, and that's why you came to Riverton, ain't it?" she coaxed, touching his arm, her red mouth curved in a bewitching smile. "Why else?"

Ki was growing aroused, but he was also growing tired of playing her game. He wondered how far he could get with her, or rather, how far she'd go for what she could get from him. She was now so close he could feel her warm breath against his face, but greedy though she was, she evidently desired him to make the initial pass. So Ki put his hand on the nape of her neck, drew her a bit lower, and kissed her. She responded with enthusiasm, the pressure of her lips like an eager promise.

He began to fondle one of her breasts. "Some folks might think, Prudence, that you were trying to turn my head."

"I'd never hope to lead the likes of you astray," she sighed, wriggling some, stroking his bare chest with her fingertips. She didn't object or become angry when he started fondling both her breasts, seeming to resign herself to being made a party to an adventure right then and there. In a minute or two she was moaning softly and Ki suggested, "Let's go to my room."

"We could be seen. Let's do it here."

"Somebody might want a bath."

"Let 'em wait their turn." Easing from his embrace,

she stripped nude with that vacant, burnt expression some women get when they're ready for sex. Ki had been wrong, in that under her dress she wore panty-drawers, tight-fitting, the drawstring digging into her belly. Her large, blackberry-nippled breasts swayed and shimmied as she tugged her drawers down, exposing a frothing mass of chocolate brown, bushy between the cheeks of her big solid rump. She was breathing hard, as though there wasn't enough air in the room when, naked, she climbed into the tub and settled down facing Ki.

"Great idea, Prudence," Ki remarked genially, as she started to run a soapy washrag over his torso. "We'll be next to godliness while we're at it."

"You guys are all the same," she said, working the cloth along his thighs. "All you ever care about is poking a girl."

"What's wrong with that?" Ki took the cloth and rubbed it up and down her legs and into her groin. "You like it, don't you?"

"Let's not discuss it," she sighed, lounging with her legs slightly bent and spread, while Ki soaped and cleansed and stirred her to feverish arousal. The brush of kneading hands across her breasts, the feathers of his fingers stroking her swelling nether lips, his gentle kiss of her nose, her earlobes, her trembling lips, all combined to evoke in the girl an erotic stupor. She raised her face and pressed her open mouth tightly against his, her hand searching down between them. Ki couldn't help gasping as the tease of her fingers closed about his throbbing erection.

"Damn me," she whispered in a low, throaty voice as she rose, stooping and turned around to face his feet, his legs stretching between hers. "All you guys aren't all the same, damn me no." Placing his taunting shaft against the opening of her moist sheath, she prodded Ki into herself with her own trembling fingers, then squatted down, swallowing the whole of him up inside her quivering belly. Leaning back against him, she purred, "This is nice."

Ki thought it was pretty good too. He could feel her body pulse as she undulated her buttocks against his pelvis, her thighs splaying to allow him greater access as she hooked her calves over the sides of the tub. He rubbed her crevice, tweaking her clitoris, his other hand massaging her breast, while she pumped smoothly upon his rod in a pressured squeeze, matched rhythmically by his strokes pistoning into her loins.

"Yesss, this is nice," she repeated shakily. "How'd you know?"

"Well, I've always found it nice before."

"I mean, how'd you know I'd be willing?"

"I don't know," Ki replied, while thrusting upward. And he didn't. How can any man know anything about a woman? Not that he gave a damn about that or anything right then, except for the exquisite pleasure building explosively within him.

In any case, his vague answer seemed to satisfy Prudence, who moved more urgently as she too neared completion. "If I'm getting too loose for you," she gasped above him, "I'll get on my knees and we can doggy-hump. That'll pinch me tighter."

Too late. Ki didn't even have time to tell her never mind, as he climaxed violently up inside her. She shuddered, convulsing, crying out orgasmically. He collapsed limply, and she lay panting, pressed firmly back against him, exhausted, satiated.

Soon Prudence yawned and climbed from the tub. A twinge of self-consciousness stole over her as she toweled dry. "I don't want to leave," she said, low and tremulous. "But I'm afraid Melvin will snitch to the owners if I'm any tardier now. I can meet you later, maybe, if you got want of me."

Ki nodded, smiling, regretfully eyeing her dress.

"You're so strong, hard. So terribly brave to've bucked Pascal just by yourself. Don't have to anymore; I'll help you. Just tell me how." She leaned over the tub and gave him a quick kiss. "You can trust me."

"Well, that depends."

"Depends?"

"On later."

Prudence looked confused. "Later? How?"

"On whether you can lead me astray any better then."

Prudence turned white. She glimpsed the laughter in Ki's face and realized he was teasing her—that he had been all along. She had bargained for nothing. "Of all the cheap—!" Her open hand cracked viciously across his cheek, and she whirled toward the door.

"Hey, Prudence," he called, "you forgot my laundry!"

The last he saw of her was the fringe of her dress against the back of her legs. Then the door slammed and he was alone. He got up and rehooked the door, but no longer felt in the mood to relax soaking, so he emptied his suit and washed it and his slippers in the tub. Then after drying off, he put on clean denims, a collarless cotton-twill shirt, and the damp slippers. His face was somber as he stowed his weapons in the many pockets of his worn leather vest.

During his bath, the hall had had its share of comings and goings and other usual noises, to which Ki paid little mind, but it chanced to be empty now when he returned to his room. More sounds filtered through while he laid his suit out to dry—until suddenly there rose a great hullabaloo of shouting and stomping. Ki's slippered feet were quiet as he stepped across to the door. He took the knob in his left hand, the haft of a dagger in his right, and eased the door open to peer out.

Then his jaw sagged. "What the hell . . . !"

• • •

Not long before, while Ki was still readying for his bath, Jessie had been preparing to go out. Right after locking her door, she sat on the edge of her bed and, sighing, tugged off her boots. The floor was cold to her feet as she padded over to lower the window blind and light the oil lamp on the bureau. She then stripped naked, filled the chipped washbowl with water from the matching pitcher, and used a hand towel to scrub herself.

Jessie would have adored to bathe and wash her hair, but sincerely doubted she'd have any chance of that before morning. Constantly rinsing out the towel, she made do by sluicing off most of the C&NW train ride that was clinging like patina to her face, limbs, breasts, and loins. She rubbed her skin to a glowing pink with the larger, if equally threadbare, bath towel. Her nude flesh tingled as she, like Ki, changed into more workaday clothes.

When she walked lithely downstairs from her room, she was wearing a plaid flannel blouse and form-hugging jeans and jacket. Her derringer was concealed behind the wide square buckle of her belt, and her pistol was now holstered at her thigh. This may not have appeared as stylish as her fashionable ensemble, but considering the circumstances, seemed much more sensible to her.

Locating an Overland Telegraph office in the C&NW depot, Jessie dispatched a cryptic message to Starbuck headquarters, advising that they had reached Riverton, and requesting a check on Oscar Pascal. The telegrapher scratched his hair while trying to decipher her garble. Yet hers couldn't be any more confusing, Jessie thought as she left, than Slats Burdou's original cable reporting the switched cows and arrested manager. The Box M foreman must be a man of few words, for he sure hadn't wasted any explaining, and reading sense of the very few he'd used had been tantamount to cracking a code.

Burdou had sent that telegram from Natrona, the local railtown for the Box M, thirty-odd miles north. The Starbuck staff first treated it routinely, for on the surface it was routine. Starbuck financed and managed hundreds of small spreads, like the Box M, which independently were losers but co-operatively proved profitable, supplying beef for Starbuck contracts, and causing chronic headaches for the head office. Then a smart clerk solved the message, realized this was no mere problem, this was TROUBLE, and bounced it up to his bosses.

It didn't take long for Jessie to be informed—after all, the Starbuck buck stopped with her. By then a detailed report and pertinent data had been amassed, convincing her that saving the Box M from bankruptcy and Hep Mulhollan from a felony charge were important enough to handle personally. Since at the time she and Ki were on business in Des Moines, a trip to the Box M, or to Fort Washakie, where Mulhollan was jailed, would be fairly simple. She asked which destination needed them more when she wired Burdou, care of Natrona's telegraph office, to expect their arrival. In answer came his cable from Riverton:

"NEED MOST HERE STOP ON CENT STOP STAY POINT CONTINENTAL HOTEL STOP HURRY FETCH STOP SLATS END MESSAGE

"Burdou knows bird-dogging," Ki had remarked while translating. "He's on the scent, not 'cent,' of something or somebody, and is holding like a pointer at that hotel for us to come bag the game he's tracked to Riverton."

That, anyway, seemed to be his claim.

Maybe the telegram was true. Maybe Burdou believed so and was wrong; or he was lying and it was a lure; or maybe it was totally fake and he wasn't even the sender. Jessie had the means to check on such things, on someone's caliber and hidden motives, however sound his reputation might be. But she hadn't the time to spare for it now. Besides, Burdou's reputation stank as bad as all the Box M crew, who were considered party to foisting ganted cull stuff on the government. To find the truth, however, was the whole purpose in their going there; yet she was also keenly aware of the perils in blind assumptions. To head straight for Riverton was a decision not lightly made.

It was made, and they'd arrived, and now Burdou was missing. Jessie began feeling a bit anxious while she plugged along searching from place to place. It was solidly dark now, with a night sky dusted by cold stars and the thin sliver of a first-quarter moon. Lantern light filtered through dirt- and smoke-rimed window panes, while the street was alive with rowdies and laborers and reservation Indians, money burning some pockets and thirst parching all throats. Jessie listened to their drawling laughter and spasmodic profanities with detached curiosity, hoping a stray word or move might help her locate Burdou, whom she'd never seen. Still, he was supposedly at dinner, and she figured that being a Box Emmer and lying doggo to boot, he'd likely keep to himself. So she concentrated on prowling the eateries for a waddy chowing alone, who was sufficently tall and gangly to merit the nickname Slats.

She discovered a few possibles, but none of them panned out. Finally when her hour was nearly over, she returned frustrated to the hotel, where the clerk informed her that moments after she'd left, Mr. Burdou had come in and had gone up to his room. Jessie climbed the stairs, her eyes flashing a peculiar greenish shade, the hue of an iceberg's edge when salt water washed it. Her father would have said she was in one of her "damned moods."

Reaching room 23, Jessie knocked on the door. She

got no answer, but seeing a bar of lamplight under the sill, she tested the knob and found the door unlocked. Easing gingerly inside, she saw she was in a room almost identical to hers, this one having a couple of empty whiskey bottles on the bureau and a man stretching out on the bed, apparently asleep. He was in his fifties, with iron-gray Dundrearie whiskers bracketing his gaunt face. He had "cowpoke" written all over him —in his work-faded hickory shirt, scuffed Justin boots, wide-brimmed hat on the bed beside him, and a walnut-stocked Colt .45 holstered in a shellbelt looped around the bedpost. His scarecrow shoulders and narrowed midriff, his saddle-bowed legs and rope-calloused hands—these things bespoke the thinned-down toughness of a born puncher who had ridden for a lifetime.

"Burdou? Slats?"

Again receiving no response, Jessie stepped over to the bed and leaned down, intending to shake Burdou awake. Then it was that she saw the stab wound in Burdou's cadaverous chest, saw the pool of blood which soaked the shirtfront. His body was still warm; he'd been killed only a short time before.

Jessie confirmed that the death of Slats Burdou had been recent when she saw that the man's blood was still welling from the knife wound over his heart, the guttering stream not yet having had time to drip down on the blanket over the cot. Death had visited directly ahead of her, damned coincidentally, and in spite of Burdou's efforts to pass unnoticed.

Obviously Burdou had been surprised and overpowered very swiftly, for the room showed no signs of a struggle. But the pockets of his butternut trousers and those of his shirt had been turned inside out, and the ruffled shape of his pillow indicated something had been pulled from under it. Stooping to peer under the bed, Jessie spotted Burdou's only luggage, a carpetbag with a padlock over its leather handles. A knife blade—the death weapon, judging by the bloodstains on the carpet-bag—had been used to slash open the bag.

It was empty.

As she straightened, a gruff voice snapped, "Heist 'em, bitch!"

Sheriff Quinby stood framed in the doorway, the barrel of his shotgun supported on his left forearm, its muzzle covering Jessie. "This's the third customer in two weeks to get knifed in this hotel," the lawman growled, indicating the corpse on the bed. "Now I tumble to who's doin' it. A greedy, blood-thirstin' slut!"

Chapter 3

Slowly Jessie raised her arms, her mind surging with thoughts.

Slats Burdou was slain, no doubt, because he'd wised onto somebody or something to do with the rustling. In that regard, anyone the killers linked to him risked the same fate, which meant she'd been foolhardy to explain her reasons for visiting Burdou, even to the sheriff. She supposed that despite Quinby seeming to be overbearing and politically opportunistic, as Ki had surmised, and too lucky with his timing to suit her—his appearance at the fight right when Pascal was losing—and his arrival here right while she was snooping struck Jessie as suspiciously convenient—the lawman was probably honest within his limits. But probably wasn't sure enough. Jessie had no intention of confiding in Quinby until she knew whether he was reliable or not.

"Don't even dream of escape. I'll blow a hole through you bigger'n the slop jug you ply your trade with," Quinby threatened, stepping into the room, nostrils twitching from the odor of blood. "Funny; we'd suspected bums, hobos, but never your kind of tramp. But looks like I got the last laugh, and got here in time to nab the Riverton Ripper smack dab after her latest kill."

"The Riverton Rip—! I cannot be your town killer, Sheriff; use your head. You saw me at the depot, you know I arrived only this evening."

"I saw you there footsyin' with the Chink who pasted

Pascal. I don't know for sure if you rode in on the afternoon train, but presumin' you did, I hazard you was returnin' to strike again."

"No, it's my first time in Riverton," Jessie argued, standing utterly still while Quinby lifted her pistol and stuck it in his belt. "It's my first time in this hotel, too, and I just came from the lobby and got here a moment before you. Ask the clerk, since you don't believe me."

"Believing stories is up to the judge. I only believe in taking no chances. Easy now; fork over the blade you used and any others."

"None." Gingerly she spread open her jacket. "See? Not any hidden. No knife in the body or the room, either, so how could I have stabbed him? I didn't, I tell you; I found him like this."

"Uh-huh. And you never cried out, never rushed for help, never turned a hair," Quinby scoffed, "though the poor sap's clothes are turned wrong side out. Lemme guess: you wasn't really riflin' his belongings, you was merely attemptin' to learn who he was, ain't that it?"

There was nothing Jessie could say to that, so she didn't try.

"If I hadn't perchanced to pass on way from m'room, you'd've skedaddled slicker'n snot, same's afore," Quinby continued, producing a pair of handcuffs. "Just for the record, who are you?"

"Starbuck. Jessica Starbuck."

Quinby gave a sardonic laugh. "Oh, sure. You floozies don't fool nobody, takin' on names of high society belles." Snapping the cuffs around Jessie's wrists, he added, "Once I rousted a whore titlin' herself Marie Antoinette," while he gestured for Jessie to walk out ahead of him.

It was then, when they were leaving, that Ki glanced from behind his door and gasped "What the hell!" under his breath. Somehow Jessie had run afoul of the same shotgun-toting lawdog as he had—accused, Ki soon gleaned, of killing the man in room 23. Slats Burdou! If Burdou's secret died with him and Jessie sat in custody, Ki realized that'd be a severe double whammy to their plans. Well, Burdou was history; Jessie was his more important and immediate concern, for worse fates than arrest could still befall her. That depended a great deal on what the sheriff did, on what he had in mind; and gauging by his pugnacious countenance, he was capable of any damn thing. In general, though, Jessie had Quinby nicely pegged, Ki thought as he overheard her protest.

"You can't be so stupid as to refuse to face facts, and you can't be as dumb to the truth as you're acting. Whatever, you are making a mistake."

"Won't be the first," Quinby growled. "And clapping you into jail till we figure decisions won't make near the mistake of lettin' you roam."

Ki glimpsed Quinby talking, scanning the hotel guests who stared curiously from doorways. He ducked behind his door, a bit relieved to hear the sheriff's intentions. Jessie was in bad trouble but not in imminent danger, apparently—blessedly, for rescuing her here and now would be lunacy.

"The baddest mistake would be by any accomplice lurking about," Quinby went on to say. "Be warned: you'll get the first round of shots."

"But—"

"Nope, I don't want to listen to no more lies." Quinby prodded Jessie to the stairs. "Me'n the coroner will come back for that poor soul's body and the evidence. You'll get your chance to speak in court."

With the long-barreled shotgun nudging her spine, Jessie was ushered down through the lobby and out of the hotel. They moved on along the street, Jessie keeping her cuffed hands discreetly folded, the sheriff remaining vigilant but not being blatant. And so inured to such sights were the night-folks of Riverton, that they gave the pair only passing notice.

Out on the boardwalk, Ki glided through the shadows, following at a ten-yard distance. He saw the lawman escort Jessie across the street and down an alley between a dance hall and a pharmacy, in the direction of the C&NW train yard. Their trail led him into the yard, where machine shops and a small roundhouse were located. The yard's sidetracks were occupied by rows of parked cars. He saw Jessie hustled around the end of one string, and on to a short spur track where a lone boxcar was standing.

An elusive shadow against the night's blackness, Ki skirted the string and then paused as he studied that single car. From the turntable two blocks beyond, the headlamp of an old 0-4-0 saddleback switch engine swept its yellow cone across the boxcar, and Ki saw that it was fitted with iron-barred windows and a ramp leading to its open side door. A jail on wheels . . .

That pretty well mirrored Jessie's opinion when she entered the car. A lantern revealed two cells, which partitioned off one end of the car. After Quinby removed the handcuffs, he locked her in the left-hand cell.

"Well." Satisfied, he drew a cheap, fat torpedo cigar from his breast pocket. "I've got m'duties to go do. Have you et?"

"Not really; not since breakfast."

"I'll see if I can get someone to fetch you some grub." Smirking, he sparked a match and lit his cigar, which to Jessie smelled as much as it looked like a dog turd. "Meanwhile, get comfy. You ain't goin' nowhere."

Quinby was right, Jessie thought as she gazed around. She was inside what appeared to be a military stockade car, surplused from the Civil War and rolled to railroad "end-o'-track" camps until no longer roadworthy. Parked and sold, then, it made a sturdy calaboose for a railtown like Riverton, cheaper than any building could have been. The cells were small and held only cots and lidded chamber pots abuzz with flies. The tiny windows and the cages themselves were barriers of latticed strap iron.

No, she certainly wasn't going anywhere for the moment. She was alive, at least. Her best chance of staying alive, she felt, lay in remaining as some unknown harlot. Burdou's killer, or killers, would dispose of her in a flash once they tumbled to her identity and connection with Burdou. Her ruse would not last long, though, and could complicate her speedy extrication from this dilemma. Cases weightier than the local garden variety could slow a frontier legal machine to a glacial pace, and Jessie could envision the endless confusion of attorneys over *Strumpet* vs. *Starbuck*. Ah well, if the law failed her, somehow she'd bust out with the aid of Ki and her derringer.

Quinby, hooking his key ring back on his belt loop, nodded curtly to Jessie and trundled the boxcar door shut. There was the snap of a massive padlock, and Jessie was left to her own dismal thoughts. Right then they were about Ki. She had hoped—indeed, half expected—Ki would show himself or even intercept them somewhere between the hotel and here, and now she was wondering what might have happened to him. . . .

Ki had decided to dog the lawdog. When Quinby emerged from the stockade car and padlocked its door, Ki's initial impulse was to wait till he left, then slip up and talk with Jessie. On second thought, to break in wouldn't be any quick or quiet trick to pull; yet to stand out halloo-ing through those high little ports wouldn't be any shrewder a stunt to try. And besides, their confab could keep. Jessie wasn't going anywhere. But Quinby was—taking off with the keys to the jail and, Ki suspected, to the murder.

The sheriff left the railroad yard and hastened back

the way he'd come, up the alley toward the main street. Ki was ten yards behind when he brushed through the batwings of the Red Devil Tavern. It was long and narrow, crudely furnished for crude customers, a roughcut mob packing the bar and tables with percentage girls, while in the rear, others clustered at card games and dice tables with eyeshaded dealers. Ki had been in meaner saloons, but only rarely.

By the time Ki entered, Quinby had sunk into the crowd seemingly without a trace. It took Ki some hard moments of hunting to spot where he'd surfaced, at a rear dice table, conversing with the table's sallow-faced croupier. Their manner gave Ki the impression that Quinby had come for something, had gotten nothing, and was demanding explanations while the dealer offered excuses. Parting, Quinby shoved toward the front, overlooking Ki in the welter as he passed at arm's length and strode out into the night.

A moment later, Ki slipped out of the Red Devil. Hastening to keep Quinby in view, he headed uptown along the boardwalk, then angled across toward a large, nondescript barn set back from the street. The barn's double doors were padlocked, the adjoining wagon yard was deserted, and the weedy lot on the barn's other side was empty, as far as could be seen.

Quinby led Ki across the lot, which extended out and around the rear of the barn. It was a dump of old empty barrels and crates, broken wagon parts, and similar refuse. In the midst of the litter, looking much a part of it, loomed a dilapidated tin-roofed shanty, tilting on a rotted foundation. Lamplight glowed through the worn shade of the cracked front window, and a couple of saddle horses stood with trailing reins near the front door.

Seeing Quinby make for the door, Ki veered in a swift detour around the rubbish heap to the rear of the shanty. The sheriff, reaching the stoop and kicking a broken harness aside, hammered on the door. Ki was an obscure shadow crouching by a side window, peering in, when the front door opened.

It was a one-room shanty, and the room was a hovel, illuminated by a flickering, sooty lamp set in the center of a heavy clawfoot table. Also on the table were unlabeled moonshine bottles, some greasy playing cards, and scattered mounds of burnt match sticks. Around the table sat three men holding cards and staring doorward, at Quinby and a fourth man, who'd obviously gotten up from the game to answer the knocking. All four were in common range garb, rumpled and dirty, and loaded with weapons. The seated three were heavyset, experienced jiggers, while the one standing was young, lanky, and badly scarred. This man Quinby now drew aside.

Ki pressed close against the window frame, watching the pair in their private huddle. The sheriff spoke mostly, gesturing in emphasis, and the young man mostly listened, nodding in response. Diligently, Ki strained to hear or lip-read, but Quinby spoke with his face averted and too low for Ki to catch his words. His actions reached Ki, though, loud and clear. Ready, wary, too aware to be startled, Ki perked up fast and fierce as he saw Quinby take a key off his key ring and give it to the man, who pocketed it. Alerted, alarmed, Ki still felt a shock, if no surprise, when he saw Quinby hand over Jessie's pistol. The young man promptly secreted it inside his shirt.

On that note, the powwow ended. Quinby opened the door and waited on the stoop while the man walked to the table and cashed in his matches. Forced by the open door to move slowly and very cautiously, Ki faded back from the window as the man, hitching his gunbelt, went and joined Quinby. Ki was almost to where he could cut off around the rubbish pile, when he heard Quinby and the man step from the stoop, a momentary snatch of talk drifting back to him.

"'. . . buck,' she spits, an' I about shat," Quinby was

saying dourly. "Who'd-a guessed? Rigged like a country hussy. She came along mindin' me, no bite, no balk, a docile doxie so long as I let her think I thunk she was one."

"A slumming siren of Satan," the young man declared.

"Maybe so, Gabriel, maybe so. For a fact, she's the Miz Starbuck pictured in weeklies, always hobnobbing with tycoons and potentates. 'Cept I nab her snooping round that dead snoopy puncher. Smacks me she's down roughing like you say, out for men, but I wager she's out for blood, out to wreck more'n to vamp. For sure she didn't come on a lark, and her snakin' around threatens us all. The rules for snakes is, catch 'em first and don't make deals."

"We must confront evil to annihilate it."

That didn't follow, Ki thought. That was also the last he could hear. The voices were now so faded he could've missed a connection. He didn't like the sound of it, though—he hadn't liked the sound of anything he'd heard—and he decided he hadn't heard wrong. The man, Gabriel, mustn't have all his cinches tight.

Gliding crouched, Ki skirted back the way he'd come. As he was swinging in from the cluttered edges of the dump, he saw that Quinby and Gabriel were already striding along the boardwalk, and after a backward glance to make sure the shanty door was closed—it was—Ki sped on a direct course across the open lot. When he had passed the barn and reached the street, he found he had lost track of the men. He sprinted down the boardwalk, craning to scan all around him, and after a few anxious moments, spotted them not too far ahead.

They were standing at an alley corner, shaking hands. Before Ki had gone another ten feet, Quinby and Gabriel had split company to head in different directions. Loping on, Ki had a second or two of indecision, as he glanced at the massive back of Sheriff Quinby moving away, and then the other way toward the scarred man named Gabriel. . . . Gabriel . . . It hit Ki then what the name connoted, how it had apparently affected the man, twisting his mind.

Gabriel: "God Is My Strength!"

Gabriel: Archangel of the Annunciation.

And now this Gabriel, a crazed perversion of the Avenging Sword of the Lord. Perhaps he was compelled by delusions, loony as a bedbug; but Ki had a hunch it was mostly an act, a rousing show leading to the execution, and allowing him to get away with murder. Whichever, Gabriel was the homicidal toady of Sheriff Quinby, and he was spearing straight toward the C&NW tracks and the stockade car where Jessie was being held prisoner.

Made reckless by a sense of danger heading Jessie's way, Ki matched Gabriel's running gait. Reaching the train yard, he moved stealthily yet swiftly across the right-of-way, his slippers making a soft abrasive sound on the clinkers. Urgency crowded him harder when he saw that saddleback switch engine on a course that would cut him off. The engine was shunting a lengthy string of empty cattle cars across the yard, on a track which lay between him on one side, and Gabriel and the stockade car on the other. Ki launched into a headlong dash to skirt the chuffing locomotive. He almost made it.

The engine beat him by a nose. Ki had to skid to a halt to avoid plunging on under the driving wheels. The saddleback switcher was a small yard beast, made for power rather than speed when new, and not having much of either anymore. The seemingly endless line of cars clicked past him at a snail's pace. Ki stood there watching the procession, clenching his fists in anguished frustration at having lost Gabriel—and consequently, at quite possibly having lost Jessie as well.

For the last glimpse Ki had of Gabriel, the killer had reached the stockade car and was mounting the cleated ramp to its door.

Chapter 4

When Jessie heard Gabriel unlocking the padlock with the sheriff's key, she assumed the sheriff had indeed returned.

As Gabriel trundled the door open, she called out, "Well, did you find out you made a mistake?"

Gabriel stepped in. "Wrestling Lucifer is never a mistake."

"A-men," Jessie replied to be sociable, and tried another idea. "Wrestling up some food isn't bad, either. Sheriff Quinby promised he'd send someone over with a meal. You wouldn't by chance be that someone?"

Gabriel's scarred face scowled imposingly in the glare of the ceiling lantern. "The Bible offers succor, not eats! Repent!"

Jessie was nonplussed. "I've nothing to repent!"

"Repent while you can!" Gun metal made a rasping sound as Gabriel pulled a .44 Starr from his holster, aiming its heavy barrel at Jessie's chest. "Repent afore I exorcise the demons from your soul. Be quick!"

Jessie thrust against the bars, beseeching, "Oh, I implore mercy!" Then slumping her shoulders, she folded her hands in front of her, thumbs hooking behind her belt buckle, and said in a woebegone voice, "I reckon I cannot cloak the sinful truth from a smart and righteous man such as yourself. Oh, pity."

Gabriel licked his lips. "I shall suffer your confession, afore you are consigned to the eternal fires of perdition."

"Try to understand, sir, I'm new to Riverton, having run out of luck up Casper way." She sighed tremulously, purposely speaking in a low, downcast tone in hope of luring the man nearer. Luckily she hadn't been searched or left handcuffed; Quinby apparently assumed she was unarmed and defenseless. But a lot of good it did being able to spring her derringer, with nobody around close enough to draw it on. "But the dance places, like the Continental Club, are all full up and don't need new talent, and I'm kind of broke, andbu3"and a girl has to make a living, y'know what I mean?"

"I was right; she's a Jezebel to the core," Gabriel muttered, with a gleam in his eye. He told her, "I know you mean you've sinned, sinned sorely."

"Yes, sir, and I wish to put my past behind me, and that includes this town. I'll never grace Riverton again, I swear. I was given that chance mere minutes before my arrest, y'know, by a gentlemanly bunch of miners who offered me their camp. Oh, outdoor solace, nature's purityMI know I'd turn over a new leaf. So, if by some chance you could see in your mercy to aid me, if you could escort me to their wagons, I'd be grateful. Ever so grateful."

"I ain't that loco! Once you get in there with all of them, I wouldn't get anything for a month of Sundays!" Gabriel backed a pace, thumbing his gunhammer. "You are the Whore of Babylon, an abomination unto the Lord!"

Jessie fell back from Gabriel's revolver, knowing that the barrier of the cell's door offered scant protection from heavy-caliber slugs. Hoping beyond hope, she snapped the derringer from the back of her buckle, even as she saw the man's rigger finger white at the knuckle. Her body quivered, awaiting the expected slam of point-blank lead tunneling into her chest—

The wick of the lantern in the stockade car jerked to the concussion of the gunshot. But Gabriel's .44 Starr had missed its intended target. A split second before, from out of the night had whirled a braided rope—actually a *surushin*, a six-foot cord with a leather-covered lead ball at each end. Flying in through the open door of the jail car, the spinning rope wrapped itself around Gabriel's head and neck. One of the lead balls smacked solidly against his right temple. It was at that instant he fired, his Starr spewing its fiery missile safely aside of Jessie.

Gasping in amazement, Jessie saw Gabriel lurch from the concussion, shock sagging his knees even as his momentum kept him upright. In a wild stagger he reeled back toward the door, his haed jerking around to face the doorway.

"Ki!"

Jessie yelled the name joyously, as she saw his welcome features limned in the lantern light. With a hoarse bawl of fear, Gabriel blundered agains the door frame and toppled backward off the top lip of the plank, fumbling to aim his revolver. Ki vaulted the ramp and dove in pursuit.

Gabriel was wheezing, stumbling on the ground, his figure a darker silhouette within the pocket of shadows there. But a lethal glint was in his eyes, and there was a firmness to his stance as he trained his revolver. Ki scarcely had an instant's grace to dart aside before the revolver lanced flame and a bullet seared along the sleeve of his left arm.

Instantly Ki lunged forward. He landed on Gabriel with the added force of a snap-kick, splintering ribs, collapsing a lung, and traumatizing the heart. Gabriel, his brain scrambled from the blow on his temple, gave a rattling cough and dropped motionless, weapon still in hand.

Ki kicked the revolver aside and hunkered, unroping Gabriel, finding him dead. Hastily he ransacked the body, retrieving Jessie's pistol and the jail key. The *sur-*

ushin he folded in half and fed through his trouser loops, fashioning an innocuous belt, slip-knotting the ends so tat the lead weights dangled like decorative baubles. He dashed back inside to Jessie, who was staring anxiously from the iron-strap lattice of her cell.

"God, Ki, thank God you're all right! This dance was too close, too close by half to being the last dance. Who was he, a maniac?" she demanded, reaching to grasp his hand through the bars. "What is going on?"

"The law; it's going on vacation." Briefly, Ki recounted the sheriff's visits to the saloon and the shanty, and of Gabriel's lethal mission. "I figure Quinby expected Gabriel to be at the Red Devil, which is the sort of dive he'd hang out at. Anyhow, Gabriel got a key and this—Ki passed Jessie her pistol—to leave behind, is my hunch, as proof you were shot while trying to escape."

Nodding grimly, Jessie then provided the details of her discovery of Burdou's body and her subsequent arrest. She wasn't surprised that Sheriff Quinby had recognized her; she wouldn't have been surprised to learn that everyone in town knew. It was just that this mysterious rustling caper was rapidly growing more complicated, grimmer and deadlier. "That double-dealing lawman will be around any time to check Gabriel's handiwork," she said apprehensively. "I must get out and we must get away, fast. Any chance that key will fit my door?"

"No," Ki said, trying it. "Your padlock's all different. Big and solid, too—hard to shatter. We could try, but at the risk of wasting all your bullets."

"Well, I'd hate to risk just waiting, hoping to waylay Quinby. Too much chance of other men being along, or of other things going wrong and his jailbreak scheme coming true."

Aware that time was fast running out, that any second might see the sheriff and perhaps a squad of deputy gunslicks, Jessie and Ki lapsed quiet as they furiously considered every possible, and impossible, solution.

Ki broke the hush, musing contemplatively, "Might be tryable . . ."

"Anything! What?"

"Recall one down-yard," he thought aloud, turning doorward.

"Ki? Ki, where're you going?"

"Seeing," he called as he left. "Maybe scrounging."

Hurrying along the jail car spur, he headed for the large sheet-metal repair shop. Soon the spur joined into a sidetrack; shortly, the track junctioned with another track, and this second track went to the repair shop by way of a tall water tower. Parked under the tower spout was that same old saddleback switcher. Its string of cars was gone, delivered wherever; but its steam was still up, the smokestack and valves making ascending clouds that disintegrated in the sharp night air.

Two men were starting to walk from the engine to the crew shack adjacent to the shop. The engineer and fireman, Ki presumed, as he evaded them and a few others and he sneaked into the shop. Lantern light was spotty, focusing brightest where the work crew was overhauling a boiler assembly, and Ki took care to stay low, silent, and in shadow while scavenging the tool racks and workbenches. When moments later he ducked out unseen, he carried a heavy hacksaw and a packet of extra blades under his vest.

As he passed the switcher on his way back Ki glimpsed a roundhouse man, a "hoghead," filling up the engine's water tank. Speedily and uneventfully he reached the stockade car and plunged back inside to Jessie.

"Here—to cut the lock," he said brusquely, handing her the hacksaw and blades, then bolting for the door. "Keep cutting no matter what!"

Before Jessie could ask any questions, Ki was gone.

This time he scooped up Gabriel's revolver and stuck it in his pants as he ran. Pausing to throw the spur's switch at the sidetrack, he rushed on to the junction's switches, and moved ahead to the switch engine. He approached softly. The hoghead was still aperch the boiler, just finishing with the water tower's spout. Nipping through steam jets hissing from the cylinder cocks, Ki seized a cabin grabrail and hoisted himself up the iron steps.

The firebox seethed, the boiler thumped and clanked, the cab sweltered with fumes of hot grease and coal. Ki knew nothing about locomotives, yet he opined that this one sounded sick, smelled worse, and looked like it had been hit by field mortars—but who cared; it worked. Now the hoghead was climbing down. Ki listened, and aside from standing very still, made no particular effort to conceal himself.

Wearing a dirty blue Mackinaw and a Scotch cap, a dark-whiskered stump of a man clambered into the cab—and drew up short. "What the devil!"

"Do you know how to run this thing?"

"Hell, yeah. I'm taking it in for an oiling now."

"No, you're coupling on to the jail car on that siding."

"You're drunk. Git off before I chuck you off!"

Ki drew the revolver. "What's your burying name?"

"Sh-Shubert, but . . ." The hoghead gulped, automatically shoving the Johnson bar in reverse. His hand trembled as he reached for the throttle lever. "You're crazy, tryin' to get away with this whopper, bub. That's Sheriff Quinby's Riverton calaboose carriage, that box."

"I'll worry about that. You get rolling."

"Sure, sure. Just keep that gun t' yourself." Shubert opened the throttle a notch, easing the switch engine up-track from the water tower. After a moment he said, "The spur's aside us, and the loco can't leapfrog tracks, y'know, so why don'tcha f'get your . . ." His voice faded as the engine rattled over switch points angling from the track and crossing the junction, linking with the sidetrack that led to the spur.

Ki smiled. "No wrong ways, no stop-offs, no tricks at switches."

Glum, the hoghead leaned out the cab window, surveying the right-of-way desperately. But there was no one within waving or hailing range; no help nearer than the shop and crew shack. The engine shuddered over the next switch point and onto the spur, which was rusty-railed and disused save for the jail car. With flanges crunched against the car, draw-bars grating and couplers hammering together.

"We'll check," Ki said, motioning with his gun. "You go first."

Climbing down, they found the coupler knuckles firmly pinned. they also discovered the jail car's stationary brake solidly clamped, and Shubert about bust a hernia trying to crack the brake wheel loose. Back up in the cab, Ki kept him relentlessly at gunpoint as he adjusted the Johnson bar, eased the brakes, and fed steam to the pistons. The stockade car reluctantly pulled free of its resting site, squealing and shaking as if with palsy.

Leaving the spur, the engine gradually gathered speed, rolling backward through the junction and dragging the car past the dark bulk of the water tower. Ahead, the track skimmed by the repair shop and crew shackMrisky, Ki knew, but so far no sign of alarm, of anyone tumbling wise. Beyond, the track merged with others to form the main line, and Ki was thinking they might yet make it there unnoticed when the door of the crew shack flew open.

Out of the shack doorway burst an infuriated man, dressed only in a flannel shirt and long underward, shaking his pants in his fist. Ki recognized him as the engineer he'd seen walking away from the switcher.

"Hey! You sonofabitch! Whatsa big idear, there—"

Ki nudged Shubert. "Yell back that it's all right."

Shubert laughed, a note hysterically. "Y'think he'd listen to me?"

Other distressed crewmen, engine wipers, and mechanics, poured out in a horde, bristling with rifles. Ki saw flashes of gunflame and billows of powder-smoke blister the darkness, and heard the clang of high-velocity slugs glancing off engine steel. The engine trundled over the main-line switch points; passed the yard limits, entering Riverton, then chuffed southward with the irate crewmen chasing after. Their rifles continued whanging away, but the distance was rapidly growing between them and the engine, and shortly they ceased firing.

"I know them guys, they've just begun. They'll stoke up the speeder that's ready in the toolhouse and overtake us lickety-split—*if* we don't blow firstest. Or get stuck plowing carnage and mayhem through town," Shubert told Ki, his face soulful, as he reached for the whistle cord. "This's only a shuttle, y'know, and was boneyarded out to us when the Chicago crew tired o' fixin' it." He pulled the cord in a strangely forelorn series of blasts.

Perfect, Ki thought sourly, eying the shimmying, jouncing stockade car. *Yes, the perfect jailbreak, expertly pulled with no one the wiser; escaping down the center of Sheriff Quinby's town, scraping Sheriff Quinby's prized hoosegow along behind*. He turned and looked out the fireman's window, down the right-of-way through the center of town. A chaos of men and horses was catapulting aside, sprawling, scrambling to get back up; while those already on the shoulders stood shaking their fists or firearms. Ki thought he heard the sound of shooting, but he couldn't be certain amid the ringer clatter of wheels, the thunderous engine, and the whistle's banshee wail.

There was no mistaking the cannon roar of an 8-gauge, 32-inch-barrel shotgun, though, or the hail of .00 buck raving through the window by the boiler head, mere inches from where Ki leaned. Flinging himself to the iron floor, he heard the swath of buck striking pipes and gauges, ricocheting off metal parts and plates, and felt bits of metal sting his cheeks. He stayed down as a few big-caliber bullets danced around in the cab. Then he crept over and peered over the flat side fuel bunker mounted behind the cab.

Sheriff Quinby was tearing down the tracks in livid pursuit, tamping afresh cartridge into his shotgun. With him, in a kind of flying wedge, were six gunmen or deputies—Ki doubted there was a difference—blazing away with pistols and Winchester saddle carbines. Ki was in no shape to fritter ammunition, but he aimed Gabriel's revolver and shot, figuring that since Gabriel had been one of them, they deserved to get what was his. One of the men close to Quinby tumbled off to the side, clutching his upper chest. That didn't seem to phase Quinby, though two more of his men slowed considerably, working their carbine levers, firing their magazines dry. Quinby raise his shotgun.

"Get down!" Ki warned Shubert.

The buckshot tornado swirled with a deafening eruption. Ki hugged the floor, hearing bullets carom off the engine from funnel stack to endplates. A couple of them punched slotes in the boiler jacket by the safety valve dome. As with the trainmen, though, the engine was gradually pulling out of range, the firing becoming more sporadic, and then tapering off.

Getting to his feet, Ki turned to order Shubert to increase speed. But his voice died in his throat. The hoghead, seizing the advantage of his opportunity, had leaped from the cab. Pouching his revolver, Ki sprang to the engineer's window to peer out. Sure enough, there was Shubert lying in the right-of-way, Sheriff Quinby slogging up to lend assistance. Their pursuit was momentarily delayed, left behind in the street.

And Ki was left alone in the cab.

Turning, he regarded the jumble of controls with misgivings. In no time flat he'd have to learn how to run the engine and, more importantly, to stop it and, most importantly, to walk away alive. Carefully he studied the maze of gauges and valves and levers on the boiler head, trying to remember how Shubert had done what to when where. He was still hard at it as the engine rumbled over the Wind River trestle south of Riverton and settled down to a jouncing clip, southwest-bound through the reservation.

By now Ki felt he recognized some of the machinery, and that Sheriff Quinby was far enough away in case matters came to a sudden halt. Reaching for the throttle bar, he jerked the lever a couple of notches on its quadrant, then hastily eased off when he felt the locomotive shudder violently. The drive wheels, responding to the surge of steam in the cylinders, began to spin on the rails without getting traction. Sparks showered into the night, the drive rods threshing impotently. Not knowing how to feed sand to the rails from the storage dome atop the boiler, Ki had to let the engine pick its own action. In doing so, it automatically picked up speed.

Wheels aflash, boiler awheeze, the old switcher stormed on backwards, hauling the relic of a jail car. Ki let it go, taking a breather from engineering to try his hand at fireman, shoveling crumbly coal from the bunker into the firebox. He knew Jessie would be working frantically with the hacksaw. He also knew Sheriff Quinby would raise the alarm back in Riverton, and the C&NW yard superintendent would gladly volunteer the use of that speeder Shubert mentioned. Another disturbing possibility occurred to Ki as he watched telegraph poles blink by the cab—that of news being wired ahead, so a posse would be waiting to arrest the train stealer.

The green eyes of sidetrack switches blurred past. But to the south, below the black, corrugated ridges through which the tracks sliced in a series of compound curves and cuts and fills, Ki caught the glow of Arapaho three miles away. Although Ki had heard about Arapaho, he'd never visited it, and had no desire to start tonight. It was on the Little Wind River and next to being on the Agie River, too, and was the base for one end of the Fort Washakie wagon road. Why Arapaho got the wagon road and Riverton got the fort's rail line, was just another peculiarity of frontier politics, Ki supposed. However, any town that's predominantly teamsters and troopers, as was Arapaho, would be one rough cob to be nabbed in.

Accordingly, he turned his attention once more to the bewildering array of levers on the boiler head. He rammed the throttle home and felt the locomotive slow down. It was gradually losing its head of steam anyway, but Ki realized the momentum might coast the switcher the remaining distance into Arapaho. And he had serious doubts he or Jessie would coast out of there quite so easily. He tested various levers without finding the brake mechanism. Pulling the Johnson bar into neutral seemed to add to the speed of the chuffing engine.

Taking a chance then, Ki thrust the Johnson bar into reverse position. Drivers screamed, the boiler cried fit to burst, and the cab vibrated like a gale-torn ship. Then, quite by accident, Ki threw the brake lever and locked the brake shoes against the drivers. The switcher grated to a halt after fifty yards of shrieking skid, which Ki was positive must have reached Quinby's ears in Riverton.

Dropping from the cab, with the panting breath of the boiler in his ears, Ki sprinted back to the jail car. The ramp had been an early casualty, torn off in transport and tossed aside like a biscuit, but the door was open, so Ki had no trouble vaulting up inside. The ceiling lantern was swinging like a pendulum in its bracket overhead. Jessie's hacksawing ceased its abrasive rasp as Ki stepped over to the cell door, noting with approval that she'd sawed much of the way through the padlock hasp.

"As an engineer, Ki, you'd make a good bronc-buster," Jessie said in mock seriousness. Her hair was awry and her left cheekbone had a bruise where she'd been thrown violently against the iron lattice. "I've been tossed around in this cell like a pair of dice in a chuck-a-luck cage."

Ki grinned ruefully, "Your arm must be tired. Give me the saw."

Jessie had worn out the blade, and Ki worked swiftly to install a new one from the packet he'd filched from the repair shop. Then he fitted the blade into the kerf which Jessie had already cut in the hasp, and resumed work. Metal dust glittered in the lamplight as the blade chewed deeper and deeper.

Jessie flexed her arm muscles and rested. When Ki paused for a moment, they heard a faint humming sound in the rails outside, an infinitesimal vibration transmitted through the stockade-car trucks to their feet. And as they exchanged glances, Jessie said grimly, "Train coming. Quinby's wolf pack didn't waste much time giving chase."

Ki, mopping his damp face with a sleeve, stepped to the car door and leaned out. To the northeast, from the direction of Riverton, a locomotive headlight stabbed the darkness, five miles away and coming fast. Jessie's escape depended on how much sawing they could do in the next five or six minutes at the most. Hurrying back to Jessie, who had taken up the saw again, Ki watched her until her cramped arm wilted completely. Ki snatched the saw from her hands and carried on the job with hardly the loss of a stroke.

The humming of the rails increased in volume. The Riverton sheriff's locomotive was out of the hills now, bearing down on the stockade car and switcher. The headlight beam threw the greasewood and boulders along the right-of-way into sharp relief.

"It's ready," Ki said, flinging the hacksaw aside as the hasp was severed. Taking Gabriel's revolver out and using the barrel for a pry, he forced the opening in the hasp. With shaking fingers, he clawed the hug padlock through the gap in the hasp.

The next moment Jessie was stepping out of the cell.

They leaped to the car door and saw the blinding yellow eye of the oncoming locomotive bearing down the tracks at slackening speed. An intervening tangent swung the headlight's beam slightly to the south, putting the stockade car doorway in momentary shadow. Seizing the opportunity to leap out of the car without being seen by the men in the oncoming locomotive, Jessie and Ki dropped to the ground. They raced up to the plow-shaped cowcatcher, crouching in the shadow between the engine and the jail car as the other locomotive ground to a steam-hissing halt a few yards uptrack.

The funneling shadow of the stockade car blackened the adjacent right-of-way now, and Jessie and Ki left the track and flung themselves into the dense underbrush which encroached on the trackbed shoulders. Twenty yards back in the brush, they hunkered down and waited, peering through the foliage.

Men were swarming out of the cab of the pursuing locomotive, converging on both sides of the stockade car. Sheriff Quinby's curse was sharp and clear as he clambered inside and spotted the corpse. "They plugged Gabriel, gents!"

"Danged if they didn't have a hacksaw, Sheriff," another voice rumbled, "with the C&NW iron on the handle. This was stole from our shops!"

Confusion inside the jail car died off momentarily as Quinby's yell knifed through the darkness. "They can't be far, men! This hasp is still hot from being sawed! Hicks, you take the east side of the tracks. Ferryman, you'n me will scout the west side."

"Sheriff," came the protesting voice of one of the men—Ki recognized it as that of the hoghead—"I knowed for a fact one is armed, and won't hesitate to make a lead honeycomb outta any of us. Chasin' owl-hoots in the dark ain't no affair o' mine."

Jessie and Ki grinned in the darkness as they heard Quinby's profanity. "You rasty-assed turds, I'm orderin' you to help hunt that fugitive couple. They're as vicious as they come! The whore killed a cow-waddy over at the Continental, which is why I jugged her. Her Chinee pimp must've shot Gabriel."

"What was Gabe doin' in your jail car?" someone demanded, and another voice piped up to add, "Yeah, didn't you say you locked it?"

Jessie chuckled. "That'll be a hard one for Quinby to answer," she whispered. "He'll pull in his horns now."

In a moment or so they saw the sheriff round the back end of the jail car, peering out across the reservation where Jessie and Ki were hiding. Indecision was in his bearing now. Tracking down an armed and desperate foe was no job to be performed on a moon-poor night. Shrugging, he turned back to the men whose legs were visible between the trucks of the jail car. "I'll roust out a posse over here when it gets light, and see if I can pick up their sign. There's no use risking an ambush tonight."

Five minutes later the two locomotives, one in reverse, were heading toward Riverton, the stockade car sandwiched between them.

"Any ideas?" Ki asked wearily, as they got to their feet in the waist-high brush.

Jessie's eyes stared at the horizon glow marking the location of Riverton, but then she turned and contemplated the dark, wild terrain westward. "Only one place to go now, Ki. Fort Washakie. I've a hunch all of this is tied up together, and we need to talk with Mulhollan and Major Thinnes before we can hope to unravel it. But," she added grimly, "I've got another hunch that before that, we'll go full circle back to Riverton, to a star-toting skunk who's got answers to the questions I'd have asked Slats Burdou. . . ."

★

Chapter 5

Midnight saw the two fugitives trudging along the wagon trail to Fort Washakie. They had avoided Arapaho, hiking overland from the railroad tracks to intercept the trail, figuring its route would be shortest and its roadbed would leave no clear sign for Quinby's posse to follow the next day. It was deserted of traffic, but they kept to the shoulders and shadows just to be safe, maintaining a steady yet unhurried pace in order to last the twenty-some miles to the fort.

After five miles, they came to a trailside clearing where three small cabins stood crammed up into each other, sharing roofs and a common chimney. It was a road ranch, they knew. Typically, one side cabin would act as a barn and stable of sorts; the other would serve as general store, swap shop, and barroom; in between would be a dwelling for the owner. They also knew that an isolated road ranch was risky at best of times, doubly so at night.

After five miles in high-heeled cowboots, though, every step was sheer torture to Jessie. Stubbornly she refused to complain, but it was obvious to them both that she'd cripple long before the fort. And being caught out lame come morning was, in balance, a greater and deadlier risk than stopping here.

Outside, the road ranch was shuttered closed, but lamplight seeped from within the barroom side, indicating activity despite—or due to—the late hour. While Jessie waited among the trees at the clearing's edge, Ki went in and drank a beer as he sized up the action. The customers were few and seemed an itinerant bunch—drifters of back-paths, strangers to one another and liking it that way. The one-eyed proprietor was more talkative, especially after Ki bought four roast beef sandwiches, peeled bills off a wad of cash, and casually mentioned a powerful need for a couple of horses.

"So happens I took trade of two good 'uns, tack 'n' all," the man confided, and when he added, "I can letcha have 'em cheap," Ki knew he was in for it.

Ki was right. Corraled behind the barn was a hock-scarred gelding and a liverish hammerhead mare, and the gear Ki was shown looked as frayed as the horses' hides. The man priced them at three times their worth; Ki countered with half that, questioning their papers; and the man offered to split the difference, arguing he checked papers and buyers with the same blind eye. Ki paid, saddled both, mounted the gelding, and led the mare over to Jessie.

"They're warm and breathing," Ki said as he returned her shrunken money roll. "Don't ask much more of them, and nothing at all of their history."

"Fine, just as long as their four hoofs touch the ground," Jessie sighed, climbing into the saddle, "and my two feet do not."

The sandwiches gave out in minutes, but the horses proved sturdier and feistier than appearances suggested, perhaps from being penned inactive. At a loping trot they rode the trail west through a region of brushy hummocks and scalloped ledges, the Little Wind River near on their left, its flow torpid and low and usually hidden by foliage. As dawn began highlighting the eastern sky, they reached the wide bowl of the upland valley containing Fort Washakie.

The trail meandered on, eventually cutting up through an unnamed sutler settlement below the fort. The settlement was a squalid hodgepodge of dingy tents, plank shanties, and sod hovels that looked like the ground had merely swollen into shack-sized tumors. They were all interconnected by rubbish-strewn footpaths among the boulders and woods on both banks of the river. At this early hour it slumbered, exhausted from raucous nightlife.

Above, the bugle-rousted fort was stirring awake. Like many such posts, it was not barricaded behind some stout palisades with ramparts and gates; it was an open encampment having the usual militia of troop billets, warehouse, stable and farrier's shed, and a centrally located commandant's headquarters. Arriving at the headquarters building, Jessie and Ki tied their horses to the already crowded hitchrail and walked inside, where they located a hall door labeled MAJOR CHESTER THINNES, C.O. A regimental lieutenant, busy checking his ration and troop strength morning reports, glanced up with an annoyed frown when they entered. It quickly melted to a vapid grin as Jessie flashed a fair-damsel-in-distress smile while approaching the wooden railing.

"Please, can we see Major Thinnes?"

"He's in conference, ma'am. Unless you've important business—"

"Ever so vital, Captain," she breathed. "Simply crucial."

"Lieutenant, ma'am, Lieutenant Pomrrit." He asked their names, wrote them down, and pointed to a partially draped alcove. "You go wait till the major's free, Miss Starbuck, then I'll get you in. I can, too; I'm his orderly."

Thanking him, Jessie and Ki went and settled themselves on a bench in the shadowed alcove. Pretty soon they heard the major's office door open. A man came out talking, his voice loud and terribly familiar.

"I caught her red-handed in Slats Burdou's hotel room," Sheriff Quinby was saying. "She's a cool bitch who'd het up any man, believe me; but her an' her Chinese fancy man are both hard, vicious murderers, deservin' no mercy."

A rumbling bass voice, with overtones of weariness, answered the Riverton lawman. "Take your report and descriptions to Colonel Benteen. He has charge of troop patrol. Standing orders are to pick up any whites unable to account for their presence, so if a pair of killers is on the loose, as you say, it's quite possible Colonel Benteen's already holding them on suspicion."

The sheriff appeared. His hand gripping the doorframe, he peered back into the office. "They won't fall easy as that. Seein' as how they escaped outside m' town limits, off somewheres across your reservation, Major, I figger the military could join in huntin' an' helpin' to capture 'em."

"The army is not a vigilante corps for civilians," Thinnes answered, sharp and somewhat miffed. "Make your report to the colonel, Quinby."

Jessie's hand was on her pistol butt as the sheriff turned. His back was to the alcove, though, and he stomped out through the hall door without seeing them. Once the door was shut, she relaxed and murmured, "He's sure an early bird."

"Not early enough to catch us worms," Ki replied, grinning.

After a moment they were beckoned by the orderly, ushered into the office, and introduced to a trim man wearing a field "undress" uniform with leaves of a major. His hair was gray and still very thick, his face sun-blackened, spade-bearded, and humorless as he arose from his desk and extended his hand.

"Major Thinnes, at your service. I've been expecting you."

Jessie blinked. "You . . . have?"

"Of course. Hep Mulhollan told me his foreman sent word you were coming on Box M's behalf," Thinnes explained, motioning them to take chairs. He was last to sit, all the while eying them thoughtfully, rubbing his lean Anglican jaw. "Small world . . . Sheriff Quinby was just in here saying the foreman died, stabbed, and demanding I field a company of troops with orders to shoot the killers on sight. He claims they're a man and woman who broke custody but, my, smaller world still, his description of the couple match you two perfectly."

Jessie glanced at Ki. "I think the major should know." Ki merely shrugged, so she eyed Thinnes and concisely related the grim events which had transpired since her arrival in Riverton with Ki the night before. "It seems Burdou's information died with him, so we're working almost blind on that part," she finished her summation. "But not quite. Quinby was too close, too quick, to not be involved, and I suspect his attempts to kill us are linked to Burdou's death as well. Other than that slight hunch, I know nothing at all about the Box M switcheroo or about what dangers, present or future, we're facing."

"Unbelievable!" Thinees sat up, concerned yet skeptical. "Quinby isn't old-maid respectable, I grant, but he isn't roped with skunks, either."

"What's unbelievable? That he's after us, wants us shot on sight?"

"Oh no, and I don't care for his ways, his bending the law to enforce it, his brutality," Thinnes said as he studied them. The imprints of their ordeal were plainly legible on their faces and clothes. He paused then, frowning, before he asked, "You're sure, now, Quinby is fully aware of who you truly are?"

"I overheard him," Ki replied. "I can't back it up, though."

"And he'd certainly deny it." Thinnes paused again, longer, then gave them a sidelong glance. "After all, you're not Chinese, are you, Ki? And no offense intended, Miss Starbuck, but you're not, ahem, a soiled dove?"

"Proof of that is easier to get," Jessie answered with a wry laugh. "But I fear I was mistaken to tell all this without hard evidence. It's not helping our own troubles any. Forget we mentioned it, please."

"Consider it done. I can't very well act on unsubstantiated charges." Thinnes stood and put on his cone-peaked hat with its crossed-rifles infantry insignia. "I can't act on unconfirmed descriptions, either, particularly when denied by parties of note. The result would be lawyers and courts and sullied reputations. As it stands, it's a regrettable case of mistaken identity. Beyond that, it's local politics, in which our policy is not to interfere."

Jessica nodded appreciatively. "Thank you, Major."

"None due, Miss Starbuck. I follow rules, not make them." With his lips quirked ever so slightly, he moved from behind his desk and thrust an arm through Jessie's. "Now, let's go look at that beef herd. Then if you don't agree that Box M tried to run a blazer on Uncle Sam, I'll eat my shirt."

They waited outside the HQ building until the orderly had brought up Major Thinnes' saddle horse. Mounting, Thinnes ordered tersely, "Lieutenant, have Adele advised to prepare lodging for two, and dispatch Sergeant Neville of Company F to the pens on the double." After that the Major maintained a stony silence as he, Jessie, and Ki rode across the parade grounds, followed a lane through the enlisted men's barracks area, and reined up before a large acreage of holding pens.

"Most of the cattle we shipped back to the Box M, but a percentage was retained for evidence," he explained, waving a hand at the bawling russet cows milling in the corrals. "There's a fair sample of the stock we received, just as it was unloaded off our rail spur."

Jessie and Ki stared. The herd was more decrepit than they could have imagined. It looked as if it had just hit the end of a thousand-mile trail drive during the drought season, not one animal in five having enough tallow under its hide to conceal its ribs. Jessie climbed over the corral fence and inspect the U.S–branded scrubs at close range. When she returned, she was shaken.

"They've got the Box M earmarks," she admitted.

Thinnes nodded soberly. "Hep insists they're not Box M beef, however," he said, then lapsed quiet while a lanky trooper rode up on a cavalry pony, drew rein alongside, and saluted. Thinnes introduced him. "Miss Starbuck, Ki, this's Sergeant Rufus Neville, the non-commissioned officer in charge of distributing army beef to the Indian agencies and our own grazing ground. Sergeant, these folks are here concerning the Box M affair."

"Yessir, glad to oblige." Sergeant Neville was in his mid forties with amiable eyes and expression offsetting rather predatory features—a vulture's curved beak for a nose and a gashlike mouth under the awning of a gray mustache. His weather-grizzled appearance, calloused hands, and saddle-warped legs marked him as a veteran cowpuncher, who for reasons best known to himself had drifted from the range into the army. Nodding to Jessie and Ki, he added, "I 'fess, I ne'er dabbed loop on ornerier steaks ahoof."

"Where," Jessie demanded, "did you first rope them?"

Neville glanced at his C.O. and caught Thinnes' nod. "At the Riverton train sidin', brung in from Natrona on the C&NW. Me'n my squad picked up the stock cars and manifest there, and shipped 'em to the fort on the army's railway that we took over from the ol' Zenoble mining syndicate."

"The cars were still sealed?"

"Yes'm. Plus, we checked the car numbers against the manifest tally sheets from Natrona," Neville affirmed emphatically. "We did what we're supposed to, is all I know, and that's all I know about the matter."

Further palaver only seemed to confirm this. Jessie and Ki learned minor details but received no revelations. They were soon out of questions, so Major Thinnes dismissed the sergeant, his face stern yet sympathetic as he then told them, "I'll take you to Hep Mulhollan now. You've seen the problem, and maybe, I think, you also can see our position."

"Well, I can't blame you in the least for rejecting the herd," Jessie said, remounting. "Have you had to reject much Box M beef before?"

"None. Always gotten top shorthorns, rolling in fat."

"Then this must've been a shock. How did Mulhollan react?"

"Apoplectic," Thinnes replied as he led the way. He gave a dry chuckle. "Normal for Hep. After four years of him furnishing the post and reservation with beef, take it from me he's a blustery rannihan. Chafes more than his share of folks, but personally, I'm Montana-born and tend to enjoy tall winds."

"I see," Jessie said, an edge to her voice. "You know a man four years, aren't cheated, and are friendly, until one bad problem, then he's the baddie. That's what I see. Sorry, Major, I cannot see your position."

Thinnes harrumphed but made no comment, waiting till they rode by a shell crib and turned onto Officer's Row. "You may not be aware, Miss Starbuck," he began hesitantly, "that the Indian agents have been complaining the past two-three years about their beef being stolen off reservation grass."

"No, but I'm not surprised. The reservation is a tempting target, and the Box M has reported that Wyoming's pestered with fast-snatching raids."

"This's been more serious. The army's Inspector-General department has been nosing around for months, secretly investigating these losses, and I.G. agents were here when Hep's shipment of scrubs arrived," Thinnes divulged. "They don't know Hep, except as boss of our largest stock supplier, and . . . Well, the I.G. boys suspicioned the stolen beef wound up on the Box M."

"So pending other charges, they arrested Mulhollan for fraud."

"The I.G. has a good case. My knowing Hep has no influence, pro or con, but within my limits I've tried to counsel him, relay messages. . . ."

They reined up in front of a whitewashed, gingerbreaded square box of a ranch home. As they crossed the yard, a blue-clad sentry on the porch jumped to attention and threw a salute. Major Thinnes took the salute as a matter of course and ordered the sentry to walk their three horses over to a stable orderly for grooming and graining. Approaching the front door, he removed his hat, his expression wry as he finished his statement.

"Since Hep Mulhollan isn't in the military, confining him to the penal brig wasn't mandatory. I put him under house arrest," Thinnes declared, opening the door. "My house."

As they entered, a woman approached from the parlor. "Ah, you've brought our guests just in time, Father," she greeted, smiling. "We're having brunch in ten minutes, and I hope everyone is simply famished."

Thinnes introduced them to his daughter Adele, and a moment was spent in polite chit-chat. That was fine by Ki, who didn't care for idle talk. But he did like the view. Adele was between Jessie's age and thirty, he judged, and perhaps like her widowed father, she had lost a husband for was definitely not spinster material. Her summery shirtwaist wrapper was light and tight enough to display her trim figure, and there was soft loveliness in her tanned features. Her eyes were a clear, deep hazel behind dark lashes. Her hair, auburn and wavy, framed the high-cheeked curve of her face. Her nose was small and straight, and her lips were full and made for smiling, though Ki soon learned they had a way of going still that warned of hidden strength in her.

Finally, in answer to her father, Adele said, "Hep is in your den; where else? Poor man's worn a path in the carpet. Do remind him we're eating."

The major's den had shelves of military books, campaign maps on the walls, and a big window overlooking a garden plot. It also contained Hep Mulhollan—six feet tall, two hundred pounds, features seamed by sun and weather, hair and mutton chops whitened by age, but still all hard bone and tough gristle. He was pacing to and fro before the window like a caged animal, and did not stop or look up immediately when Jessie and Ki were ushered in.

"Mr. Mulhollan?"

"Speaking to him." Mulhollan's voice was vibrant and low-pitched.

"I'm Jessica Starbuck," she said, and introduced Ki.

Mulhollan stopped and looked then, his red-rimmed gray eyes snapping from Jessie to Ki. "Wal, whiffle my tree," he declared, his face brightening. "Thanks for comin' like you promised, Miss Starbuck and, er, Ki. I apologize and accept responsibility for things slippin' so poorly outta hand."

"Please, call me Jessie," she replied, hoping informality would ease his strain. "And don't take blame for troubles not of your doing."

"Miss Jessie, I swear on my oath I never bum-steered the army. I loaded the pick of my roundup at Natrona," he declared vehemently, "and that's what I'm replacin' them scrawny mosshorns with, to the last hoof and horn. My foreman is leading another range gather for the Box M's primest stock, and should be shippin' 'em to the fort any day now."

"Your foreman, Mr. Mulhollan—"

"Hep, Miss Jessie. By all holy, I never saw that herd of stove-in cows before. I'd bet my last blue chip they never chewed a cud of Box M grass. Yet they wore the underbit and crop earmarks that're registered to the Box M, and were branded with a U.S. iron, like we use under supervision of quartermaster inspectors. I dunno, Miss Jessie, I dunno how you or anybody can help me figure my way clear of that."

"This won't help," she sighed, and informed him of Burdou's murder.

The news was like a body blow to Mulhollan. All the fire and bluster in the man drained from him as he stared in anguish. "Who killed Slats?"

Jessie, again sensing truth to be her best weapon, repeated the story.

"I don't know what Slats was after, what he might've found," Mulhollan then said dazedly, sinking into the nearest chair. "I didn't even know he was going to Riverton." He buried his head in his hands, elbows on the chair arms. It was obvious from his expression that he was grief-stricken, but had accepted her account and innocence at face value.

In turn, Jessie and Ki accepted Mulhollan the same way.

Ten minute later, the Thinneses' housekeeper had spread a table with steaming food, set in front of the French doors, which dominated the dining room. Mulhollan had lost his appetite, but had regained his voice, if not his humor. He showed qualms about discussing his plight in front of Major Thinnes and Adele, both of whom seemed supportive, and the brunch quickly developed into a council of war as various theories and plans were explored.

At last Jessie remarked, "The I.G. investigators assume you shipped the scrub stock, Hep. We'll work on the assumption you didn't, and that the Box M beef was substituted somehow, somewhere between Natrona and the fort. So next, I think, Ki and I should take a hike along the entire trackline."

"Miss Starbuck, rustlers wouldn't have nerve to heist

a government train travelin' over the reservation," Major Thinnes declared. "It's a cinch any switch must've happened north of the junction at Riverton."

"Wal, m'boys already scouted to there an' came up croppers," Mulhollan stated moodily. "P'raps that's why Slats was stopped at Riverton."

"Perhaps. Perhaps your waddies overlooked something," Ki said, adding gently, "Or perhaps one of them sold out, or was planted in your bunkhouse as a spy, and misled the others. We can't afford to ignore any possibility, Hep, no matter how slight. That's also why we've got to backtrack from here, where the shipment was off-loaded, and search every inch of the way for clues."

Jessie nodded her agreement. "We'll need an escort, Major. I wouldn't want Colonel Benteen to arrest us, or Quinby to get away with shooting us down."

"I'll go," Adele offered.

"No, it's a job for my troopers," Thinnes responded.

"That may be so, Major, and I'm sure you've implicit trust in your men," Jessie said. "On the other hand, Ki's point about Box M's crew is well taken here, too. It wouldn't be the first time an outlaw worked in uniform."

"Much as it pains, I hafta admit we sign a portion of scapegraces. Most end up deserting rather than knuckle to army discipline, but . . ." Thinnes drummed the table with his fingers. "If there are any rustlers in my command, they'd probably be in the Third Platoon of F Company. It handles the shipping and distributing of beef to the Indian agencies under our jurisdiction, and is made up of former cowhands like Sergeant Neville. Well, maybe not exactly like him; rumor has it that Neville was a jump ahead of the law for stock thievery when he enlisted. But his service record is clean, and I won't cast aspersions against him or anyone who may've joined to shake trouble, any more than I drew unwarranted conclusions about you. Still, I see your point. It'd be tragic to inadvertently team you up with an army owlhoot."

Adele straightened and breathed deeply. "That settles it. I'm the only who's well known and knows the area, so I'll accompany Jessie and Ki."

Thinnes sighed the sigh of fathers plagued by daughters.

"If anything happened to either of you gals while you're working on my behalf, I'd have your deaths on my conscience forever." Mulhollan laced his hands together, thumbs rotating over each other, his slate-gray eyes morosely surveying the women. "I never thought I'd live to see the day when Hep Mulhollan would hafta holler for help, and then hafta take it from a flock o' females, but I'm elsewise stumped. I sure can't buck Uncle Sam by myself!"

Chapter 6

The Wind River basin stood out in gaunt relief under the blaze of early afternoon sun as the three riders gigged their horses out along the rails linking Fort Washakie to Riverton.

Jessie and Ki carried army-issue Spencer carbines and slicker-wrapped bedrolls, which Major Thinnes had loaned as "surplus" to them. Adele rode a similarly equipped cavalry pony and, like Jessie, had taken to wearing men's clothes. On her, like on Jessie, somehow the striped cotton shirt and slick leather leggings lost all their masculinity.

Consulting a government survery map that Adele had brought along, Jessie had no difficulty in gaining a perspective of their route as they followed the trackline. It crossed the basin to a broken-tooth line of buttes that flanked the Wind River—the northern boundary of the reservation—and then wriggled southeasterly through the hills, following the water's course to Riverton.

They kept a keen eye out as they traversed the basin, but it was a fairly straight run. There were no side tracks forking off, no private docks or loading chutes, not even a water tank stop along the right-of-way. They reached the foot of the buttes without finding any sign of the means by which rustlers could have halted the fort-bound train, stolen prime cattle out of sealed cars, and replaced them with cull stock bearing identical markings.

The tracks now curved eastward and entered a patch

of hogback knolls, like a bunched series of rocky knuckles, scrubby and encrusted. The riders pushed steadily onward, flanking the cinder-ballasted roadbed, detouring into the nearby boulders only once, when the smoke of a locomotive was sighted back behind. From the concealment of a brushy pocket above the rails, they saw a common Forney 4-4-T shortline locomotive drawing a string of Quartermaster Corps ration cars from Fort Washakie. The train was making a routine haul for supplies, they realized, and did not pose any direct threat; nonetheless, they preferred to stay unseen and go unreported.

The rails were still humming when they rode down out of the brush and rounded the next sweeping bend to catch sight of a spur track due ahead. There the rails coming from Riverton formed a Y fork; one branch angling to Fort Washakie, the other heading on into the rugged hills farther upriver. Approaching the rusty frogs beside the padlocked switch, Ki dismounted and began checking around, while Jessie and Adele scanned the weed-grown tracks that snaked off and vanished among the contours of the uplands beyond.

"I believe this went to a mine," Adele commented.

"Sergeant Neville mentioned the railway was taken over from an old mining syndicate, the . . . Zenoble, if I recall." Jessie unfolded the map and swiftly located the abandoned mine diggings. "Yes, here it is; about six miles away, with a little short piece listed on the map as 'ruins of tunnel.' "

Remounting, Ki said, "I'd like to look up that way."

"I'm curious, too," Jessie agreed. As they left the Fort Washakie line and started along the abandoned branch, she remarked, "I haven't heard of any silver or gold deposits in this region. If those're what Zenoble was digging for, I can understand why the syndicate failed."

Adele laughed. "No, they were mining natron—

crude sodium carbonate decahydrate. Everybody was, it seemed, years ago when the raw material was important to the chemical industry. Zenoble built a rail to Riverton in those early days, before the reservation and long before the C&NW, but like everybody else had to ship the natron back east. That's far—too far—to go. Boy, did it collapse once soda ash made from salt was found as a replacement."

Continuing, they entered a twisty ravine between two foothill ridges. Ki was plodding in slow fits and starts, leaning low as he scrutinized the right-of-way. Jessie was content to amble apace, unquestioning, respecting his concentration, and figuring he'd talk when he'd something to tell. Adele didn't know Ki, wasn't aware of his moods. Ringbits jingled as her pony danced sideways, wanting to romp, and soft leather creaked as the woman shifted her weight in the saddle to stare at Ki. A slight frown creased her forehead.

"This road hasn't been used in ages," she said impatiently. "I'm at a loss to gather why studying it has any bearing on the rustling case."

Ki straightened in his saddle and turned to Adele. "Notice how the rails are in a fair state of repair. There's not been a real break so far, and the crossties haven't weathered too badly either, in the time since Zenoble was operating."

"Nothing to disturb them. They're just rusting away."

"Adele, look closer. The rails are rust-pitted, okay; but their surface rust is ground in; the buildup is not as flaky and powdery as it should be. Now, what'd cause that if not something—a handcar maybe—being run over this track since the spring rains?"

"Run to where? The switch and the padlock were corroded from disuse."

"So they seemed, with their smear of dirt, soot, and cowdung."

"That's an old trick, used to antique wood, but . . ."

Adele flushed under her tan, but her full, rich mouth smiled faintly. "I stand corrected, Ki."

They rode higher through a series of corrugated hills which forced the railway into a series of loop curves. While Ki examined the roadbed, Jessie squinted off through the afternoon glare, her hands on her saddlehorn. Her eyes chanced to focus on a glint of light midway up a slope northeast of the tracks, and then, faint to her ears, came the bleating of grazing sheep. A moment later she caught sight of a mottled gray band of woollies moving along the crest of the slope. Focusing intently, she perceived a wisp of smoke trailing from the stovepipe chimney of a stone shack.

"Some sort of cabin's up there," she noted. "And a windmill."

"Lance Puheska's place," Adele answered.

"The horses could use a drink. Do you think riders out after cattle might bum water at a sheepherder's?"

Adele gave an amused laugh. "Lance won't make a fuss."

Sheepdogs barked a greeting as the saddle-weary trio approached the cabin and grounds. They noticed a neatness unusual about most such outfits—clean windows, curtains, no litter, and a native flower bed of shooting star, spurred columbine, globeflower and Jacob's ladder.

"A woman's here," Ki remarked.

"Perhaps, but not permanently," Adele replied dryly. "Lance has never been, ah, wedded to his ways."

Reining up to let their horses drink at the windmill trough, they saw a tall, angular man walk from the cabin, casually toting an old Henry .44 rifle as if it were an extension of his arm. Nearing, it became apparent he was a half-breed. Handsome enough, not much older than Jessie, he had a wiry yet strong frame that could have used some fattening, and wore work clothes that were well-worn but in clean repair. His features were sharp, deeply bronzed, smooth-skinned save for laughter wrinkles framing his eyes—lazy ebony eyes, under long reddish-brown hair. He was straight-faced, though, when he reached the windmill and spoke with that clipped, somber accent of mission schooling.

"How."

Jessie would soon wonder why she didn't catch on immediately. At the moment, as Adele introduced them, it simply crossed Jessie's mind that she'd met scads of Indians and none before had ever said *how.* Or *ugh.* Politely she commented, "This's certainly pleasant and very well tended here."

"A natural give and take, Miss Starbuck. I'm part Shoshone. I try to get along with these hills where I was born and grew and was shepherding before there was any reservation." Puheska pointed his rifle at the tracks. "My father taught me that to take, take, and never give, will eventually cost dearly."

"He was a miner?" Ki asked.

Puheska nodded. "Pit chief, back when the Zenoble was shipping regularly on that road. Until, I remember as a child, until the cave-in. Now as one of many dead, he rides the haunted horse at the dark of the moon."

"Cave-in?" Jessie prompted. "A mine shaft collapsed?"

"It was the main tunnel that landslid apart, blocking the exits. Bottled up the engine and a string of ore cars; killed the train crew and all the miners on that shift, including my dad. Zenoble closed, left them buried."

Adele regarded Puheska quizzically. "And they ride the what?"

"The haunted horse. That iron horse of their avalanche grave," Puheska explained soberly. "Two, three times a year it gets steam up. I've heard the exhaust a-chuffing and the drivers hammering those rusty rails. Even heard it whistle once, in the distance, like the lonely bay of an orphan coyote."

Strangely enough, Jessie saw nothing humorous in the 'breed's narrative of a phantom locomotive emerging from its tunnel sepulcher, with a ghost crew and a cargo of damned souls. "While it's light, would you go with us to the mine?" she asked Puheska. "I'd like you to show us around the cave-in."

"No!" he snapped. "I won't tamper with that tomb."

"Ha'nted iron horses, indeed." Adele humphed irritably. "You don't really believe in such silly Indian superstitions, do you, Lance?"

"Indian! That's the white man in me, Miss Thinnes," he retorted, turning on his heel. "My Shoshone side thinks it's hooey, but it also feels my father's resting place should stay at rest. S'long." With a wave of his rifle, Lance Puheska strode away, back toward his cabin.

Eyeing his retreating back, Jessie mulled over what he'd said and how he'd said it. Then came the dawning. "He kept totally deadpan, and was pulling our legs the entire time!" She started to chuckle, and her chuckling proved contagious. Laughter, bubbling, spilled over till the three were rocking in their saddles.

Gradually their mirth subsided. Adele straightened on her horse and asked, "Then you're not interested in the mine anymore, are you?"

"On the contrary," Jessie said. "Lance may've been spoofing us, but he may've provided us with a most important clue."

She did not elaborate, and Adele elected against needling with questions this time. By now the horses were finished drinking, so they headed down the slope to the railroad tracks. Just before they rounded the curve to put Lance Puheska's cabin out of sight behind them, they heard the echoing reverberations of a train on the main line back below, and they hipped around in their saddles. They couldn't see the train itself, of course, but following the pluming smoke, they quickly recognized it must be the army supply train returning to Fort Washakie. They also glimpsed Puheska skylined on the ridge where his sheep were grazing, standing where he could watch them head into forbidden ghost territory.

In silence the three rode on, their horses wading through patches of Russian thistles which matted the crossties in patches. The tracks wove into the hills, and other than on occasional trestles, it climbed in compound curves engineered to maintain a steady three percent gradient. It was getting along in the afternoon, and the brooding rimlines closed in about them, as stark as the crags of a dead planet. Eventually the railway crested and followed a weed-choked level that had been dug and blasted along the pit of a cliff-hemmed ravine, which gradually narrowed until it ended in a blind box of sheer rock.

Indistinctly through the shadows of encroaching dusk, they made out the tumbled ruins of the Zenoble workings. The main shafthouse had lost its roof. Brush had rooted in the mounds of tailings. The tracks headed straight into the black maw of a tunnel, which pierced the box end of the canyon. Heaps of fractured talus lay sprawled on either side of the tunnel mouth, and the pyramidal slope above showed the scars of the avalanche that had choked this end decades before.

"Look at that loose rock," Adele said, pointing it out. "That proves a rockslide shut the tunnel here. I wouldn't doubt a similar slide stoppered the far end, too, sealing in men and a train."

Jessie nodded. "Personally, I'm ready to accept Lance's story as true—except for the haunted horse business. Maybe we have drawn a blank."

Ki said nothing. He skirted great piles of tailings and passed the rusted remains of an ore car lying on its side. There, diligently, he followed the tracks as they ran to the tunnel. His horse's forehoof struck sparks suddenly and he swung down and bent to feel the rail. Then he sighted along to the tunnel mouth, which was no longer hidden in avalanche debris. Calling over Jessie and Adele, he pointed out the unobstructed view into the tunnel bore.

"It can't be the wrong hole. The Army survey map shows only one on the spur, but lists it as a ruin. But this tunnel's been cleared, you see?"

"Then what became of the train, Ki?" Adele asked. "Or do you figure that Lance just made it up as a hook for his haunted horse yarn?"

Ki shrugged and began a swift foraging for twigs and dried branches that had collected on the ground with the dust of ages. He then caught up with the two women, who were already leading their horses into the tunnel.

The arched rock walls amplified the clop of steel-shod hoofs as they entered the passage. Quickly the light grayed, the shadows deepened, until by twelve feet in it was cold as an ice house and dark as sin. Ki struck a match and lit the bunch of twigs and branches he'd gathered, having held off till now because he knew they'd burn rapidly and he wanted to make good use of them.

Guided by his makeshift torch, they continued along the tunnel. Their shadows were grotesque against the timber-shored walls, which glowed ruddy in the flickering light. Moving forward to where the tunnel made a slight right turn, they made a discovery which set quick excitement flaring through them. Almost obscured by the inky, clotted depths beyond was the front end of an old-fashioned railroad locomotive. Reflected torch-glow made the oil-burning headlight lens glint like a bloodshot eye. The stack was the flaring funnel type, the cowcatcher low and sharply angled, the boiler head scabby with rust.

"The haunted horse!"

They hastened up to where the locomotive crouched like a brooding idol in a niche. Ki swept his torch along the red-painted drive wheels, inspecting the condition of the relic engine and discovering it was not junk but useable machinery. He hoisted himself into the cab, glanced at the tender ricked high with cordwood to fuel the engine, then peered into the firebox, where he found cold yet not so old ashes in the grates.

"Lance Puheska might not have been joking when he said he'd heard the haunted horse," Ki said, grinning as he dropped trackside. "Whoever removed the slide to open the tunnel must have found the locomotive in decent repair—enough so that its boiler could be stoked and steam fed to its long-idle cylinders. This engine has been run recently."

The torch was flaming lower, growing a bit hot to handle, as they made their way along the tender and found that it was coupled to a string of stock cars. The smell of cattle and moldy straw still clung to the empty cars. They could see that originally the cars had been short-sided gondolas for the transport of ore, and that timbers, still retaining their new yellow look, had been built on the car beds to form slatted walls and flat roofs. For a hundred yards they counted cars, one hooked after another. Then they passed the tail end of the empty cattle train, and the torch went out in a smoky crumble of embers.

"I don't care," Jessie said in the darkness. "I see more light than I have since we began, Ki. Before this night is over, I believe we'll have cracked the riddle of Hep Mulhollan's vanished herd."

"Are we going back now?" Adele asked hopefully.

"Maybe not quite yet," Ki replied. "If the engine was run out the front door, I'd hazard the cows were run out the rear door. Let's see if it's open."

They picked their way onward through the Stygian gloom of the tunnel, allowing their horses to take their time, confident their instincts would warn them of any obstruction or pitfall. They strained their own ears to catch any sound that might indicate someone's approach, but all they heard were their bootfalls and hoofbeats echoing hollowly from the rocky walls and roof of the passage. For what seemed like an eternity, they pursued the resonating tunnel through the blackness until the shadows ahead began to become gray. Finally, they discerned a faint spot of light which steadily grew larger. They redoubled their caution, peering and listening, as the light grew stronger.

After a few more minutes, they passed from under a low arch, their eyes slitting to the glare of sunlight as they emerged from the northwest end of the tunnel. They found themselves on a wide ledge that faced north like an exposed rafter on the end of a half-pitch roof—an ancient geological fault which was enclosed behind and to the sides by striated cliffs. A few rail-lengths ahead, the tracks ended in a twisted bowtie. A loading chute had been built parallel to the roadbed, and beyond, in a bowl-shaped depression, were holding pens of yellow pine poles.

A trail led from the corral and dipped from the ledge. It was scuffed with a multitude of hoofprints; some of cattle, others of shod horses. The trail descended in a series of curves, many of them switch-backs, maintaining a reasonable grade for animals to go down or come up, and crossed the Wind River below in what appeared to be a fairly shallow ford. Yonder on the north stretched the tawny-peaked Owl Creek Mountains, waning sunset smearing their rimline flanks, illuminating the valley flow which spread, scalloped and corrugated, beyond the river. They could see dots of grazing cattle and faint smoke patterns from the chimneys of scattered ranches. There was no sign of movement. The silence was unbroken save for the murmur of rushing water in the Wind River below.

"Now can we go back?" Adele asked anxiously.

"Well, I suppose," Jessie replied thoughtfully, heading instead toward the trail where it left the corral. "I wouldn't mind going on, though. If I locate the Box M herd, the army will have to drop its charges against Hep."

Pausing, she scanned her expanded vista of hill and valley—and gasped, breathless. Farther off behind the pens, almost invisible against the open range of the valley proper, Jessie now glimpsed the dim outline of tents. Smoke lifted from vent flaps, disappearing against the eventide sky, and only a few cracks of light showed through unclosed slits of several of the tents.

Jessie was turning to caution the others, when she heard a twig snap somewhere on a nearby slope. She stiffened, motionless, hand about her pistol butt, as a hard voice commanded, "Hold it! Yuh move, yuh die."

Ki and Adele also froze at their unseen challenger's order.

The westering sun threw an elongated shadow across the rough ground—the shadow of a man clutching a rifle. A little avalanche of rubble peppered down the bank as their unseen challenger skidded toward the ledge. Then came the sound of spurred boots as he moved into their line of vision, sidling around in front of the horses, holding a Winchester at hip level. He was a seedy cowpoke. His lantern-jawed face was stubbled with a week's growth of beard, and his slitted eyes glittered like chips of blue rock. His long-barreled weapon swung to cover each of them in turn.

"Put that down," Adele demanded indignantly. "You've no right—"

"Shaddup!" Threateningly, he jabbed his rifle. "Now, y'all shuck."

Shrugging, Ki showed he was carrying no sidearm. Neither was Adele, who glanced frustratedly at the carbine in her saddle scabbard. Jessie drew her pistol carefully, using the tips of her fingers, and she was just tossing it aside when another six men emerged from the rocks behind the pens. She glared as they approached, hooking her hands on her belt buckle. Like the first man, they wore grubby puncher garb and aimed rifles or revolvers as though itching for an excuse to shoot. And the one looking most ready, in fact downright eager, to trigger a triple kill was none other than the mackinaw-clad, ruddy-whiskered Oscar Pascal.

"Wal, wouldja see what dropped in," Pascal brayed derisively. "Good catch, Moulton. I'd hate for 'em to go as unannounced as they came."

"It were easy, boss, snaggin' two mopsies and a no-gun slanteye."

"All 'em wogs uses hatchets and stuff," a thin, chinless man said.

The shortest of them swaggered up to Ki. "Yeah, I betcha he's hiding somethin' in his vest." He started tugging at it, aided by a tall, balding man. "Take your damn vest off, damn you—chop-chop!"

Provoked, Ki growled, "Chop-chop, eh?" Twisting to pull the bald man between him and the closest pointing gun barrels, Ki whacked the short man in the neck and in the gut, axing the calloused edge of his right palm like a shearing cleaver. "There's chop-chop!" Gagging, the short man reeled back, flattening himself and two others to the ground. Ki, meanwhile, shifted and dipped so that the bald man teetered sidewards. Then Ki catapulted him up and over in a floating hip throw. The man arced upside-down and collided with the short guy and his pals as they were just wobbling upright. They all collapsed in a swearing tangle, while the remaining men leaped in to gang up on Ki.

Again Ki stabbed with his right hand, this time spearing stiffened fingers into someone's brisket. With his left he struck at another man in a *nakadata-ippon-ken,* or middle-knuckle punch, to the throat. The results were agonized grunts and scuffled stumblings, yet even as Ki pivoted to press his attack, Pascal lunged in, lashing with his revolver. Seeing the looming rush, Ki tried to duck and twist away, but he lacked sufficient space to elude the blow, and Pascal clubbed his head with stunning force.

Blundering, almost backing out, Ki sank, dazed and bleeding, to his knees. The gunmen swarmed over him before he could recover, wrenching his vest off, kicking and scuffing him until Pascal called them off, laughing cruelly. Slowly Ki stuggled to his feet, weakened, still woozy from the pistol-whipping.

"For five years I've waited for this," Pascal chortled, rubbing a thumb along his broken hump of a nose. "Okay, boys, bring the gals," he ordered contemptuously. "You know where—same spot I'm taking this squinty bastard."

Pascal fisted both his revolvers, and he and his gunmen prodded their captives away from the pens and on past the tunnel mouth. They entered the scrub at the other side of the level, where thorny vines and briars clawed at their clothes as they wound single-file up a rockly defile. Ki had begun to regain his senses by now, though he continued to stagger groggily on purpose. Jessie walked without giving resistance, without showing defiance, while her mind worked swiftly on how and when to make her stand. She couldn't tell if Adele was thinking along those same lines, or was thinking of anything much at all. The woman was trudging woodenly, her face a mask of numb dread.

After some thirty yards, they reached a clearing at the foot of an eroded granite scarp. In the background were two rows of grave mounds, which were merely heaped cairns of splintered rock overgrown by weeds. Pascal, calling a halt, crossed to where a rusty shovel was stuck like a grave marker at the end of one of the mounds. Holstering his revolvers to free his hands, he began to wriggle the shovel loose while his men continued to cover the hapless trio.

"What an odd cemetery," Jessie noted, gazing about.

"Ours," Moulton responded, scratching his lantern jaw. "Kinda ours. Here's where we planted all the bones and stuff we found when we was clearin' the inside o' the tunnel durin' spring o' last year."

Ki asked Pascal, "Wasn't that before you got out of jail?"

"So? M'boys were busy," Pascal replied as he returned. "Doin' what, now, that's a secret Hep Mulhollan an' the army would die to know, and you'll die without knowing." He handed Ki the shovel. "Dig."

Taking the shovel, Ki considered it as a weapon. He glanced fleetingly at Jessie and Adele; then considered the weapons holding them at bay, and started to dig. Under the thin top layer of soil, the shovel struck hardpan, and his digging became more difficult. The evening lengthened; sweat soaked Ki's shirt and rivuleted down his face, stinging his eyes.

At the end of an hour, he had gouged a three-by-six pit to the depth of a foot. It was then that a rustling sound in the thorny brush beyond the clearing caught his attention. He turned his head and glimpsed a curly-bearded man approaching from the defile, leading their three horses by the reins. The man wore a shabby, brass-buttoned cavalry uniform with the insignia of Fort Washakie's Tenth Cavalry pinned to his greasy campaign hat.

"Hey, what'll we do with these mounts?" the cavalryman demanded.

"Add 'em to our cavvy, Reno," Pascal snapped, glancing over his shoulder. He regarded Ki again. "Keep digging!"

"Let the women go, and I promise no trouble."

"Trouble, Ki?" Pascal stepped to Adele and jammed a gun muzzle against her temple, laughing harshly as she shuddered in mute terror. "What trouble?"

Ki continued digging. His every instinct cried out for

reprisal, for a chance to whip the outlaw, as he had done once, five years before. But things were different now. Six gunmen grouped around, appearing bored and holding their weapons laxly. Yet they were capable of quick-trigger reflexes. The cavalryman with the horses stood at the edge of the cemetery, lazily spitting tobacco juice into the weeds. Pascal watched Ki as alertly as ever, keeping his twin S&W .44's trained and taking no chances that any of his prisoners might attempt a break.

When the grave was a foot deeper and wider, Pascal said, "Enough. It might be crowded, but don't worry, Ki, you won't feel squozed for long."

"Boss, set loose the women," the chinless man suggested.

"Squeamish, Fritz?"

"Naw. I don't wanna waste loose women, is all."

Two other gunmen chuckled snidely, but Pascal scowled at the joker. "We're not animals," he snarled. "'Sides, that's what females count on, to wheedle and sucker yuh, to set yuh up for a back-stabbin'. They're plumb natural deadlier than males."

Listening, Ki knew he'd failed. There'd be no reprieve for Jessie and Adele; they'd be shot firing-squad style and dumped in a mass grave with him, to be covered over and never found again. So he'd nothing to lose, either. He rubbed his hands along the rough wooden handle of the shovel, knowing also that whatever he was going to do, he'd have to do it in the next few seconds.

"Now!" Pascal barked, as if reading Ki's thoughts.

Ki felt himself driven forward by a savage kick in the spine. The shovel wrenched from his grip as he pitched headlong into the shallow pit. By the time he regained his feet, he saw that the women had been hurled bodily in as well. Adele was stumbling in despair, speechless and glass-eyed with mounting horror. Jessie was rising from her knees, her fingers delving behind her belt buckle, her face ashen yet braced for the shock of tearing lead.

And Ki heard Pascal order loudly above his men's obscene jeers, "Drill the bitches quick'n neat, boys, like you would heifers. But Ki is my meat, an' I'm gonna plug him in the gut and bury him alive. It was because of Ki that I spent almost five years in prison, goddamn him!"

Pascal tightened his trigger fingers on both revolvers . . .

Chapter 7

Then all of a sudden—

From somewhere higher up the slope came the jolting bellow of a heavy-caliber rifle. Simultaneously, Moulton seemed to explode at the seams. The gunman crumpled into the grave with half his skull blasted off, killed instantly a split second before Pascal could send Ki to eternity. Everybody stared in stunned, stupefied disbelief.

Everybody except Ki, that is.

Ki had no more idea than anyone else what was happening, but he'd been on the lookout for a diversion, any diversion, and this one was a beaut. He dove across the pit, a thunderous flash erupting before him as a startled and rattled Pascal triggered. The heavy .44 slug whispered harmlessly past his ear. Before Pascal could shoot again, before any of his men fired their own weapons, Ki had swung up out of the shallow pit and leaped at Pascal.

The distance was short but the confusion was great. Pascal, rearing, tripped on himself and unexpectedly stumbled awry at the last possible second, while the chinless man named Fritz thoughtlessly zigged when he should have zagged and lurched into the way. Ki drove into Fritz with flying kicks to the face and chest. The heel of one foot smashed between Fritz's upper lip and nostrils with a ramming upward thrust, shattering his nose and spearing shards of bone and cartilage into his brain. This, while Ki's other foot was crushing his ribs into his lungs and rupturing his stomach and kidneys. Fritz was dead before he hit the ground.

In the mere seconds it took for Ki to attack, gunsmoke eddied from the rocks above the cemetery, wreathing the statuesque figure of Lance Puheska astride a horse. While below, Jessie and Adele had scrambled to the near side and were boosting each other up out of the open grave, Jessie clutching her two-shot derringer in her right hand. Bullets were buzzing close around as Pascal and his gunmen triggered lead in a haphazard if concerted roar, trying desperately to kill the Shoshone above and the Oriental among them.

Both warriors were fast on the move and hard to target. Puheska was lunging hell-bent for a broken neck down the slope, his eyes as blood-chillingly wild as his war whoops, his long hair standing up like the roach of an angry wolf. His splotched paint stallion was snorting fire, sure-footedly responding to the slightest twitch of Puheska's knees or reins. Puheska shifted the reins to one hand while he checked his Henry and drew bead on Oscar Pascal. Pascal was not easy to track either, twisting and turning as he sprinted toward the cavalryman, who was trying to hold the increasingly skittish horses.

Ki, landing atop Fritz, used the body as a springboard to attack the short gunman. A bullet clipped his shirt as he pivoted in midair. Jessie shot the balding man in the chest before he could center Ki again in his pistol sights; then she and Adele raced on for their horses, determined somehow to stop Pascal from stealing them.

As the balding man folded, Ki lashed out with another kick and slammed the short man in the solar plexus. Clutching his hemorrhaging belly, the short man fell to his knees, mimicking yet another gunman who'd just crumpled hunched over as though he was praying, a fat .44 from Puheska's rifle having bored through his larynx. The gunman had been running with Pascal, and had caught the slug intended for his boss. The Henry roared and bucked against Lance Puheska's shoulder, but Oscar Pascal seemed to lead a charmed life, bullets skimming and slashing about him as he wisely detoured from the horses and dove into the bushes. The cavalryman, no less nervous than the horses, looped their reins on a low branch and plunged pell-mell after Pascal.

Jessie and Adele darted along the fringe of the cemetery, then pushed through to the horses. Ki angled off to intercept them, leaving a wake of carnage behind. Puheska was yelling like a banshee as he broke open the rifle, but before he could reload, Pascal and the cavalryman had vanished in the undergrowth, loping in frantic getaway. Jessie was vaulting into her saddle and Adele had a foot poised in one stirrup when Ki closed to grab his fractious gelding.

"Ki!" Adele cried, dropping from the stirrup. "Look out!"

Jessie too caught the wink of steel as the sixth gunman burst from the fringes for a point-blank shot at Ki. She fired her second and final bullet, which creased the man's shoulder but didn't stop him. Frantically Adele scooped up and threw a large rock, which beaned him smack in the middle of the forehead. Cussing in shock and pain, the man rocked back on his boot heels. That gave Ki the time he needed. He sprang, using a forward snap-kick followed by a sideways elbow smash to cave in the gunman's ribs and stop his heart.

"Ride!" Puheska urged impatiently. "Ride!"

Adele mounted. Ki had a momentary delay while he fought his spooked, rearing horse, but finally he hurled himself into the saddle and jabbed both heels into the horse's panting flanks. His hock-scarred gelding tore off in a lather.

Down the defile they galloped, all too aware they were heading toward Pascal's outlaw camp. They had to brave it, though, and charged back out on the broad ledge as if they were running a gantlet, which in most respects they were. In one perilous respect they were not—you don't stop midway through a gantlet. But once they'd spurred past the tunnel mouth and reached where they had been taken prisoner, they reined in hard and dismounted.

Hastily they searched the dark ground in ever-widening circles. Ki's vest was relatively easy to spot, but Jessie's revolver proved elusive for anxious moments. "I'm terrified," Adele admitted to Ki as they hunted. "Not as terrified as I was up at the graveyard, but I'm still terrified."

"You're doing great," Ki assured her, grinning.

Then, from the direction of the railway tunnel, a sharp cry rang out—that of Pascal himself. "C'mon, dammit, I want more o' you muckers in here!"

"Lord, now they're on both sides of us," Adele hissed, her eyes bright with fear and excitement. "We've got to go before we're discovered!"

"But not back, not by the tunnel," Ki said. "It's a trap now."

"Got it!" Jessie whispered loudly, retrieving her pistol.

A voice called out from the loading chutes, "Whazzat? Whozere?"

There was a drawn-out moment of silence, as the challenger halted in his tracks to play possum. Then the orange flash of a muzzle blast cut the darkness and Jessie felt a bullet sing by her ear.

Her Colt pistol came up as she realized the gun flash must have silhouetted one if not all of their crouching forms to the gunmen. She tripped her gunhammer, shooting at the smudge of gunsmoke ten yards ahead, and heard the slug thud into its target. The sound was followed by a gurgling moan. "Curly bought it!" someone else shouted. "It's them, o'er there! Get em!"

Gunfire began spewing in their direction, as gunmen poured out into the night from the tunnel behind them and the tents ahead of them. Scuttling on all fours to avoid the seething line of fire, they hit saddles and slapped lash, whipping carbines from their saddle scabbards. There was only one possible path of escape left open—the cattle trail from the pens down the hill and across the Wind River. They bent over their horses' withers, and the animals chewed up the ground as they headed for the trail, exposed on the open ledge in a raging crossfire. Volleys sizzled from the blackness, and a handful of gunmen broke from the pens and came rushing forward with guns blazing to cut them off.

Lance Puheska swiveled and his Henry spat flame. A man dropped and another cursed. Joining Lance, Jessie fired with deadly precision, then Adele downed another, and that pretty well scattered the initial charge of Pascal's men. The thundering battle continued unabated, though—pistols bucking, lead searching, horses galloping for that dropoff of the trail, their riders bracing against the expected punch of lead through their flesh.

Yet in the dark, bloody confusion, the quartet managed to reach the trail and plunge downward at a death-defying clip. A quick, shouted uproar and the blood-cry of pursuit rose from the ledge, and the gunmen began roweling their mounts after the fleeing four. Shots snarled, but the swaying riders couldn't aim effectively; their bullets were off target, high and wild.

Yet the targets ahead were exposed on the steeply slanting hill, and it'd only be a matter of time before some chunk of lead scored a bullseye. Slugs sang and ricocheted around the four as they tore zig-zagging down the slope. A bullet showered pieces of stone in Ki's face, and he ducked reflexively, feeling a shard stab into his neck. He ignored it, peering at the stone ridgings and rough brakes of the unfamiliar terrain, and toward the choppy, rapid-strewn river they had still to cross.

The white-water torrent was bedded with fanged

rocks, and the far bank was a tall bluff gashed with numerous side gullies. The trail led to the one practical ford, where the far bank dipped in a rounded, sway-backed slope. Here the river was slightly wider, appearing to swirl in gentler swells between the base of a long series of cascades and the beginning angle of a sharp curve. Obviously the gunmen were well aware that this ford was the only course available, for the darkness was alive with their gunflame homing in on the route, as they rushed to intercept the four before they could reach the opposite bank and scatter.

Out into the shallows the four goaded their mounts. The riverbed slanted acutely, and the sluicing current soon rose horse-belly high. On they plunged, hooking their knees over their pommels in case they or their horses were forced to swim, expecting to be suddenly dunked at any second as slugs bit the water and snapped in the air like fangs closing about them.

At midstream, Adele's cavalry pony took a bad stumble. For a breathless moment they feared it was going down, bullet-wounded or leg-injured, but with deft handling and some staggering, her pony recovered, apparently unharmed. They forged ahead, relieved, till something popped like a pebble on a tight drumhead, and Puheska's paint reared, screaming and thrashing the water.

"He's hit!" Puheska yelled, wrestling for control.

Jessie, who chanced to be nearest, wheeled her mare so abruptly that they skidded sideward and teetered, about to flop over. Regaining a balance of sorts, Jessie angled toward Puheska across the line of fire, gesturing strenuously at Adele and Ki to press onward.

"No!" Ki objected, turning. "I can't—"

"You can't help any; not if you're shot and need help!" Jessie argued above the dim of gunblasts. "Keep going! Get ashore and cover us!"

That sounded more sensible than it was, she realized,

aware the bank was too far to make it practical. By the time Ki and Adele could reach there and begin covering, Jessie figured, if she and Lance were still out in the river, well . . . they wouldn't be in need of any covering, except by coffin lids. So be it. Ki and Adele would be safe. Unless Ki smelled her ploy, that is, and balked at going out of obstinate loyalty and contrary male pride. That was his lookout. The split second she'd spent in responding to Ki was all the time she could spare him. Her mind focused on Lance Puheska as she slewed in closer, bullets coming ever closer, close enough to singe hair.

Rider and horse were united in struggle—a struggle so intense, so personal, that Jessie almost felt she was intruding. They fought their last battle together, the stallion faltering, sliding broadside from the force of the surging water. Puheska, wincing, reeled as if to topple, revealing to Jessie's dismay a blood-soaked gash on the right thigh of his pånts. More blood was leaking out from the wound underneath. He and his stallion wavered, defeated yet refusing to surrender, resisting to the bitter end, as the horse kneeled and Puheska looked ready to ride him beyond the veil.

"My hand!" Jessie called out. "Grab my hand!"

In a stunning display of horsemanship, Puheska gauged his paint's final breath and threw himself clear by rolling back over the sinking animal's rump. He caught Jessie's outstretched hand, seemingly without looking, and whipped up and around behind her, almost braining Jessie with his rifle, which he'd managed to hold on to.

Jessie shifted in the saddle, roweling her spurs. "Hang on!"

"I never fall," Puheska retorted, then almost did. Slipping, rocking, his rifle wobbling precariously, he groped furiously with his free left hand for some steadying buttress and, not surprisingly, latched on to Jessie.

Onto her left breast, to be exact.

Startled, Jessie sat straight up, momentarily speechless. Puheska was not kneading or mauling; he was simply cupping her breast as if unaware or unconcerned what he was using for support. Jessie was very aware. Her shock quickly waned, and she was about to protest when Puheska finished settling and dropped his hand. So she dropped her fuss, not very concerned, really. Not in comparison to the gunmen surging after them, firing more wildly than ever.

Moments later, they hit the bank at the base of the ford, almost floundering as they fought for a hold on the slick earth. Ki was a few lengths ahead, Adele slightly in front of him; they both glanced back anxiously at the slower hammerhead nag straining wobble-gaited and awheeze under the double load of Jessie and Puheska.

Again Ki turned, anxious to intercept them. This time Puheska motioned to go on, to leave them, and Jessie yelled across, "We'll split up, confuse 'em! I'll head downriver, and if any follow us instead of you, I'll ditch em!"

Adamantly Ki shook his head, aware of the sacrifice Jessie was trying to pull, and deeply fearing she might just succeed in getting martyred for her trouble. But he could not get to Jessie, short of committing suicide, for he was stymied by the withering barrage of gunfire sieving the wide-open flat between them. Lead spanged and howled off the boulders and scrub trees fringing the bank and ford, the majority of slugs having spun in past Jessie and Puheska, some whistling overhead, others geysering dust right under the mare's hammering hoofs.

Jessie yelled, "You two ride to the fort! Get help!"

Her expression anxious and apprehensive, Adele reluctantly nodded. It was the best idea of a bad lot, though she knew Jessie and Lance's chances of survival were remote even if she and Ki made Fort Washakie. With a wave, she launched her pony into a wild gallop up the cattle trail from the ford. Ki glanced at Adele, then at Jessie, swore bitterly, then took the only choice open to him by tearing after Adele, figuring she was making a wide sweep that would eventually bring them back to the river and thence to the fort.

Jessie and Puheska peeled off to make tracks downriver. Behind them the Wind River appeared choked with riders, their revolvers and rifles blasting away in erratic though massive volleys. Just to keep the pursuing mob respectful, Puheska twisted around and triggered his Henry. Three stabs of flame leaped from his rifle, three sharp reports blending as one—and three stupified men fell writhing from their saddles.

How Lance chambered so quickly, or kept his perch against the recoil, were mysteries to Jessie—but then, most everything about the man was a mystery to her. She had formed an initial impression of him as intelligent, more learned in woodlore than in schooling, and thoroughly devoted to the welfare of this remote region. And having the devil's own sense of humor. His ethics were simple; his beliefs were not, for spiritualism was complex in both white man and red, and Puheska may have combined some of each. She also suspected that, like so many decent, proud 'breeds, he had much internal conflict. He must bow to the laws of the Shoshone Lodge, but he could not accept its ways; he went to the white man's school, but could not drink whiskey as a white man does. Nor could he go where he goes or live as he lives. Lance was a man who must find out who he was. And being a mystery to himself made him all the more intriguing a mystery to Jessie, piquing her interest and personal attraction, and . . . to be honest, an awareness budded from his hand on her breast that bordered on sexual arousal. Not that she had any such designs in mind, she thought hastily; her only desires were to escape, to eat, and to sleep. And at the moment, to escape was her passion.

With that in mind, Jessie peered back and saw that they had opened a lead on the gunmen. By inexplicably splitting up at the ford, they had indeed discombobulated the men, more than Jessie would've supposed. Still, it was a temporary delay. The gunmen quickly divided into two parties, the smaller bunch swerving downriver after them. When Puheska suddenly emptied three saddles, though, it took a lot of steam out of their charge, everyone slowing, pulling rein. Nobody was eager to be in front. They were still chasing, though, still winging salvoes of avenging lead, and Jessie knew if they stuck true to form, they'd soon pick up the pace and return to their old bloodlust frenzy.

Deciding to take advantage of the opportunity while she could, Jessie pushed her worn-out mare into a mad gallop to increase the distance. It was a bone-jarring ride. The horse moved with all the smooth glide and coordination of a threshing machine. Puheska scrunched in tighter behind Jessie, clasping her firmly around the waist with one arm. They outran the bullets; they outran sight of the gang; but the hammerhead was lathering as if with shaving soap and blowing like a penny-whistle. Lance leaned forward and said into Jessie's tender coral-pink ear, "Are you Apache? You eat the raw guts once you kill her?"

Jessie gave a laugh and checked the horse to a trot. "I don't run horses to death, Lance. I wouldn't now, except we may not be able to shake the gunmen again, and I don't want them to see where we cut off from the river." She paused, gazing at the brushy fissures and jumbled rock formations of the eroded bank, a texture of blacks and shadowed grays under the dark quarter-moon sky. "Problem is, I haven't seen any cut-off I'd care to risk. Either the bank is too steep to climb, or too high, or both. And it overhangs to boot. Or it loops low alongside bouldered towers that'd make a mountain goat blanch, or opens on barren flats where anything bigger'n a field mouse would show up starkers."

"There's an area further ahead. Not the best, but it should work."

"Let's hope. I . . . I'm sorry your horse died, Lance."

"My horse lives, Miss Starbuck."

"Jessie."

"Miss Jessie. It lives as long as anyone who remembers it lives."

"I sometimes think that's the way it is with my father. At times he's so strong, so clear in my mind that I expect him to come out this door or call me to that room." She shivered, breaking her reverie. "Speaking of living, we should do something soon as able about your hole in your leg. Bullet?"

"Oh . . . yes, a bullet. Bleeds like hell, but I don't feel it much."

"Numb. When the shock wears off, you'll feel it. I'm sorry about that too, Lance. So far, anyway, the only one hit is the Samaritan who saved our collective bacon. Why'd you come? You swore you'd never go anywhere near."

"Mm. As teacher saves errant pupil, so I had to save you scoffers. Now you learn, only death awaits those who flag the Haunted Horse on the dark—"

"Bullsh—eh, shoe. You'll pulling my leg again."

"Nice leg," Puheska remarked offhand. Then he jerked as a bullet whined by. Glancing behind, they glimpsed the dark moving bulge of tight-knit riders heading their way. Jessie raked her spurs, and the weary hammerhead bolted straight downstream as a torrent of bullets pursued them. Puheska swiveled around and sighted his Henry, but, muttering about long range and few cartridges, he turned forward and hugged Jessie around her waist. They both were acutely aware that the mare was tuckering, and the mob of gunmen behind them was gaining.

"Well, at least they'll be coming into range," Puheska remarked philosophically. "Miss Jessie, I didn't have a set purpose for going to the mine. I've avoided it; I won't go into the reasons why, except to say the area mightily offends me. But after you left my place, I got to thinking of my ghost yarn and the looks on your faces, and I got curious about what train it was I'd heard. I went to join you; got the idea of maybe a prank or two first, and went up around the back way. Up till then, I also couldn't shake the feeling that y'all were in trouble. Although I still don't know why."

"I don't either, not entirely. But we've learned a few things," Jessie said, and related the events which had led to this point. "You noticed that Pascal had a cavalryman with him. I suspect he's a deserter by the condition of his uniform, but it also backs a hunch that rustlers may be hiding in bluecoats over at Fort Washakie. Moreover, it ties in with the railway and the cattle trail. Locate Pascal's spread, and one gets you ten we locate those Box M steers that were meant for the reservation."

"Pascal routed rather than face a crazy red man's rifle," Puheska murmured, feeling bullets clip past. "Now he's routed us, with reinforcements!"

"And they're on fresh mounts, and we're on . . ." Jessie slit her throat with her finger.

Now slugs began snapping around Jessie and Puheska as the gunmen started to close their range. Lead plowed the dirt at their feet and spanged off the rocks protruding from the bank. As they rode past a place where the wall of the bank had crumbled, Puheska directed Jessie that way, and she sent the mare scrambling up the pile of loose rock and into the flanking undergrowth.

The dozen or so gunmen riddled the underbrush with gunfire. The darkness was alive with the snap and whine of bullets. Rugged rocks and spurs loomed closer again. Scanning fiercely, Puheska again drew Jessie's attention, this time to the dark mouth of a narrow canyon. Its stone walls loomed high, offering shelter that the river course and fields could not, although Jessie was leery that it might be a box that would trap them.

Jessie bent low over her horse's withers, hoping the flagging animal wouldn't give out under them. Suddenly she stiffened. "Lance? Lance, what're you doing?"

What he was doing was cupping her breast again. This was no damned "error" like the first time! In one fell swoop he had his hand slid up the front of her shirt, and she could feel his thumb and forefinger rolling her nipple, tweaking it into hardness.

"Stop it, Lance! Lance?"

If Puheska had anything to say for himself, he had no chance to tell it, as the pursuing gunmen sent a raging salvo their way. Jessie sensed a slight tremor of response to Puheska's caresses, but choked it down, concentrating instead on eluding the riders who were trying to cut them off before they could reach the refuge of the rocks. Stuttering volleys of lead chased after them as they plunged into the canyon. It made a turn, then another, and the slopes grew steeper. They saw a slim gully off to one side and veered into its narrow mouth, then twisted up into the rocks. Knowing it would be rank folly to try hiding at this point, they continued climbing the steep grade, setting off a minor avalanche of loose shale and gravel.

Just before they cleared the crest, they glimpsed the gunmen reaching the base of the long slope. The men started up but were forced to wrench aside to avoid the tumbling rockslide. The horses skewed and fishtailed, bucking back down. The gunmen swore luridly. The mare pawed its way to the top of the rimline and, panting, paused for a moment to catch its breath.

"Ride!" Puheska urged. "Here isn't safe."

Jessie prodded the horse moving. "I'm not sure anywhere is safe with you."

"True, true," he murmured, his lips brushing her ear. "It's all this excitement. Makes you exciting, makes me excited."

"All it makes me is scared," she countered. "Scared and dirty and very tired." Yet she could feel perversely erotic throbs tingling up through her flesh as he continued stroking her gently, gently . . . until, despite herself, she moaned softly, having little inclination and absolutely no time to resist his fingers while they rode on into the wild fastness of the hills. She knew the gunmen would catch up again, and was determined not to make it sooner than need be by diverting her attention to Lance, but kept focused on avoiding open ground and skylines, clinging instead to rock and brush. Especially brush. And shortly, as they wound along the jagged slopes, the brush grew heavy with briars and thorny weeds.

The sound of crashing horses came through to them from their right, toward the valley. They dove into the briar thickets as the horses trampled nearer, the riders peppering shadows with enraged abandon. Jessie pleaded and cajoled and pummeled her mare on through the stinging thorns and nettles. Behind them was total chaos—shouts, the whinnying of balky horses, the uneven rattle of gunfire. Thwarted from entering the briars, the gunmen tore off around to hit their quarry coming out, but they were too late. Chased by scattered shots, Jessie and Puheska were blurs drumming into yonder roughlands. The shots did not cease until they were long out of sight and range.

After another quarter-mile, Jessie slowed and let the exhausted mare seek its own pace. Heart pounding, she listened to the gunmen fade in the wrong direction, feeling less worried now about pursuit, and stirred by Lance to a feverish arousal. His fingers were kneading one sensitive breast, then the other, teasing her hardening nipples. His gentle kissing of her earlobe and the nape of her neck combined with the ministrations of his fingers to evoke in her an erotic stupor. She found herself watery and trembly when, forging through an acreage of brush and briar, they came upon a small clearing where the dirt was too hard to sustain even the meagerest of thistles.

"I think we lost them," Puheska said. "For a while."

"You bastard," she moaned, slumping from the saddle. "You bastard, you got me gasping like a spavined mule."

Puheska chuckled, then sagged to the ground, gritting his teeth as fresh blood welled from the wound in his thigh.

Jessie bent quickly. "We'll have to get you to a doctor. All I can do now is to clean the wound and stop the bleeding." To get at the thigh wound, she had to open his pants. Her hands dealt surely with the buttons of his fly, and he raised his hips to allow her to slip them down. Then he sank flat with a low, short grunt. Jessie, staring with something akin to trepidation, wondered if his grunt was of pain from his wound, or of relief from her releasing his big, stiff, crotch-trapped erection.

The wound proved to be quite minor, a clean furrow of the sort that bleeds profusely without much injury. Using the field aid kit supplied at the fort, Jessie wadded and bound his wound with gauze bandage, determined to ignore his jutting manhood, but finding it as hard for her as it was hard for him . . . and worse, just as she was done, she accidently brushed his meaty shaft.

He groaned. "Now you're pulling my leg." Then, tugging her to him, he pressed his lips tightly against hers. The kiss was long. He ended it gradually, holding her tight before letting her go.

Trembling, Jessie said, "I don't know why I let you do that."

"You wanted it," Puheska said, grinning. "And you know it."

"That's not so," she protested, eyes fever-bright. "I'm not excited. I told you, I'm scared, tired, and dirty."

"You can't sleep or wash now, and your fear is natural. It sharpens your senses," he murmured in a husky voice that sent chills along her spine. "We're alert, aware, alone for this one short time. Why not do as we feel?"

Something prompted Jessie to gaze fully at him—something she sensed rather than reasoned; something in his presence, in his ebon eyes as they took their slow, bold fill of her, in his touch as he drew her down to him again. And as their lips melted together once more, she knew she was no longer tired. Why not? She wanted him and they were staying a while. She was caught up in an electric frenzy that seared a fiery path along her nerves. They kissed again, and again, lingeringly. . . .

Almost before she was fully aware of it, Puheska was undressing her. Jessie felt mesmerized. She would have been unable to fight his dexterous fingers even if she'd wanted to, as he peeled her jacket and shirt off and fondled her naked breasts. Garment by garment they stripped nude. Then they stretched out on their impromptu bed of clothing, Jessie stroking between his thighs, Puheska caressing her soft, flaxen curls and tender nether lips.

Buttocks tightening, Jessie arched her pelvis against his prowling fingers. Her liquid eyes closed and a gentle sigh escaped from her mouth as he rubbed her sensitive cleft, sliding a finger inside her. He slipped a second finger in, and she gasped with pleasure, her body undulating in response to his hand while he massaged her flesh to yearning arousal.

"I . . . I'm ready," she mewed. "But, but your wound . . ."

"Climb on. It is the squaw's place to do the work."

Jessie rose squatting and straddled his hips, feeling

his hot length burning against her crotch. She reached under with her right hand and grasped him, positioning his thick crown between her moist crevice, her loins absorbing his stabbing shaft as she lowered herself slowly yet eagerly upon it. Her stiffened nipples and aching breasts flattened against his muscular chest while she impaled herself completely, until the last inch of him was driven, throbbing, deep up inside her belly.

He asked, "Too much? Hurt?"

"Yes . . . *no!*" Jessie wriggled on him and felt his swollen girth flexing within her. She began sliding on him, slowly at first, then with increasing enthusiasm as the sensations intensified. Soon she was rearing high until his erection was almost totally exposed, then plunging down to ensheath him fully, gasping, trembling, as his shaft surged into her depths like a fleshy bludgeon.

Puheska shifted one hand to massage her jiggling breasts, toying harshly with her nipples. In turn, she lowered her head and their mouths fused together, their tongues touching and flicking in play. Her pounding thighs matched his pumping upthrusts, her moist channel squeezing, squeezing, while he pummeled her with spiraling delight.

"Ohh Lance!" she chanted, enraptured. "Lance, oh Lance!"

"I am! I am!"

He was spearing higher and faster into her moist passage. She shivered and moaned, quickening tempestuously, sensing her orgasm gathering tensely. Then Jessie felt his thrusting manhood swell, saw his eyes sparkle with the lusting urgency that drove him on. He was gasping hoarsely with imminent climax when Jessie cried out her own delirious peak, her fingers clawing his chest with wanton ecstasy.

"Ahhhh . . . !"

Like a bucking bronco, she arched and plunged, feeling Puheska vibrant and huge as he geysered up into her depths. His hands were on her buttocks, squeezing and relaxing, squeezing and relaxing, as though to help milk his pulsating eruptions . . .

Finally, with a sigh of satiation, Jessie slithered forward, releasing his deflating erection. He wrapped his arms around her in an affectionate hug and she pressed tighter, stifling a contented yawn. "Just for a few minutes," she murmured. "Then we'll get dressed again . . ."

For a while they just lay quietly, nuzzling and trading lazy kisses. Jessie hadn't lied to him; she'd been tired. Despite that, he'd managed to stoke her fires to a blazing pitch, to an inferno that had consumed them both. But now, in the aftermath, the fires were banked, and she nestled lethargically in his embrace. Yet Puheska grew strangely restless . . . and then she felt his flaccid girth regaining hardness and length.

"Oh, my God," she moaned, quivering. She was drained, enervated, yet as Puheska began a gentle thrusting against her, she found that her loins were responding in kind. "You'll rut me to death. Will you eat my raw guts then?"

"Not exactly what I'd in mind."

She began undulating responsively, her clitoris tingling with each pushing impact against his reviving shaft. He kissed her lips, her cheeks, and the tender hollow of her neck. Then he slipped lower, darting his tongue across her nipples, moving it wetly along her abdomen, rekindling passions within her belly. Then still lower, his lips probing and exploring as she whimpered, her fingers tangling in his hair while he worked down and thrust deep into her inner flesh. Her thighs clenched spasmodically around his laving tongue and nibbling lips, tendrils of arousal rippling up from her loins.

Puheska pressed closer and reached up with both

hands to play with her breasts, his mouth becoming a hot, hungry invader, laving with his tongue, nipping with his lips and teeth. She began to pant explosively, her groin grinding against his face with pulsing tension . . . a tremoring like the advance of a sundering earthquake. Again she poised breathless, tensing, straining—

Puheska broke free and rose on an elbow. "Someone's coming."

"Me, dammit!"

In a scrambling leap, Puheska grabbed his rifle. Jessie stared, trembling and frustrated, snapping as he vaulted toward the fringe of the clearing, "Why, that wound doesn't hurt you at all!"

"I told you I didn't much feel it." He hunkered, listening. "Riders approaching, I hear the horses."

"Lying won't help you! You knew it was a scratch, and you tricked me into dropping your trousers—" Jessie stopped, able to catch the sounds of saddle gear and movement through underbrush. The sensual spell shattered, she bolted up. "Who are they? Pascal's gang?"

"Nope! Adele and Ki!"

Frantically they sprang for their clothes.

"Where're my pants?" Jessie cried. "Of all the fool times!"

Puheska had to laugh. "Be thankful. A couple of minutes earlier or later, and we'd never have heard them!"

Chapter 8

"Don't shoot!" Ki called softly, to avoid mistake.

The underbrush parted, and into the clearing walked Ki, leading his horse, followed by Adele, astride her pony. A moment was spent acknowledging one another, with surprise and relief and a few explanations tossed in.

"We got blocked at the river," Adele said. "After we shook our pursuit, we spotted outlaws covering the only crossing points and the few hill paths on the other side. Plenty more are out and about hunting, so we decided we'd better find what'd become of you guys, and hope we weren't too late."

"You could *never* have been *too* late," Puheska replied deadpan, evading a shin-kick from Jessie as he returned to the edge of the clearing. While stuffing an errant shirttail into his pants, he studied their backtrail and remarked, "I'm more worried we were too easy to find. How did you know where we were?"

"Ki did, don't ask me how," Adele answered. "But having watched him, I suspect he could name the color of a horse from the shape of its print."

Jessie nodded. "Believe it, Lance. We weren't careless. Scouts and others who know will swear Ki can cold-track a blowfly across the Rockies."

"I'm no bloodhound," Ki retorted, disliking such flattery. Tracking to him was just common sense, experience, and close attention to details and habits; but irked by the exaggerations, he added facetiously, "Finding this hiding place was simple. Since the gunmen hadn't caught you, you couldn't be where they were; so I simply looked where they weren't." It was then Ki noticed Puheska stuffing in the shirttail and, glancing back at Jessie, saw that she didn't have her left boot on snugly. And he figured maybe he shouldn't ask a natural question like, "What've you been doing?" So instead he hastened on with, "How we got here isn't the problem. Where we'll go from here; that's the problem."

"Go strike at a known target," Puheska advised.

Adele laughed. "A snap! There's any number between us and the fort."

"But only one that counts, Pascal," Jessie said. "He might be anyplace. Even if we knew, we lack surprise, speed, and firepower to hit him. Horses, too. They're spent, and my mare's bent like a hoop from carrying double."

"I'll share my saddle," Ki offered. "Okay, Lance? *Lance?*"

Puheska was gone.

A moment before he'd been standing at the edge of the clearing. Jessie dashed to the spot, catching a slight ripple of foliage, a soft rustle of brush beyond, as the sole indications of his departing presence. "I don't like it!" she called after him. If Puheska heard her, he didn't acknowledge, but swiftly faded, invisible and silent, into the enshrouding night darkness.

"Probably Lance felt like you did at the ford, Jessie, and took off in order not to jeopardize us," Ki suggested mildly. "Or maybe he thought we're hindering him. I've a hunch he can manage better alone and afoot than with us."

"I'm sure that's right," Adele agreed. "Lance wouldn't run out on us. He had his reasons but didn't want to argue."

Jessie grumped irritably, "I still don't have to like it." She walked back and stood with a thoughtful expression, until after a long moment she mulled aloud, "Go strike at a known target. . . . If he had anything specific in mind, I'm damned if I know what it was. The fort's cut off. Pascal's got us cut off, and may well cover his traces and get in the clear, before we can grab him and some solid evidence . . ." Her lips quirked in a steely smile. "My, whatever ails me? I almost overlooked that paragon of lawdom, Sheriff Quinby."

"Smart notion," Ki said approvingly. "We're already on a downstream heading and shouldn't have great trouble getting to Riverton. And considering Quinby used us for targets, I guess we're due a return strike or two."

"How'll this help catch Pascal and his rustlers?" Adele asked.

"I'm not sure," Jessie replied candidly. "But Sheriff Quinby has been cahooting with them—of that I'm convinced. And I aim to make him sing answers if I have to ram questions down his throat with my gun barrel."

They rode without speaking much, alternately cantering their horses and slowing them to a walk to conserve energy. Now and then they'd glance over their shoulders, but saw nothing on their trail, except for once when Ki thought he'd glimpsed a smudge like pluming dust high against the night sky. If real, the haze merely indicated their pursuers were falling further behind.

After clearing a series of rubbled knolls, they found that the winding culverts grew gradually shallower and the ridges more rounded, until along about midnight they reached a broad, gently rolling tableland. Quickening their pace a trifle, they moved on across the range and shortly came upon a cattle trail. Not very wide nor well used, it came in from the west-northwest and curved toward them down the flat, then dog-legged and ran on generally in the same direction they were going.

They joined the trail, sticking to its dusty and

churned earth ruts as added precaution against pursuit. It wandered easterly through a succession of interconnecting draws and stony fields, and eventually tapered away into the mouth of a narrow canyon. Following, they entered the canyon and were rounding a bend when they smelled woodsmoke and the odor of frying meat.

Reflexively, Jessie's mouth began to water and the nape of her neck tingled with a warning nerve-crawl. "We'd better walk," she whispered, dismounting. "Whether we go on or go back, we've got to tread softly."

Leading the horses with hands over their muzzles to stifle nickering, they eased around the bend and saw the old slab hut of a line camp set on a fold of ground against the canyon wall. A squirrel tail of smoke was rising from a bent stovepipe on its roof, and four horses were tethered in a wooded clump near its closed plank door.

"Beyond the hut, the trail is like a passage," Adele murmured, "perhaps the only practical one bridging this line of hills. That would be luck!"

"Bad," Ki growled, "but not as bad as chancing into some rear guard pack of rustlers." Cursing the dead end and the wasted time it represented, he went off into a dark cleft to take a leak before they started the long way back.

Adele frowned at Jessie. "We can go by. They're just line riders."

"Possibly. This is private ranchland, isn't it?"

"Yes. I don't know who owns it, though."

"Well, do you know any rancher whose line crew would be up at this hour? Not out nighthawking, but inside cooking? No? Well, we don't either."

Drawn by his low chickadee whistle, they saw Ki motioning them over to the shadowy cleft. Joining him, and told to listen hard, they heard the faint but distant lowing of cattle emanate from the cleft, the plaintive bawl resonating hollowly out of the black depths that Ki had just irrigated.

"I think the cows are ahead, past the canyon," Ki said. "Evidently the cleft walls are well placed for catching and megaphoning sounds from there."

"Fantastic," Jessie teased. "Did the cows keep you company?"

"The whole while. And they're still restless. Come on, let's go see."

"Go on? Not back?" Adele gasped exasperatedly. "You refused to go when I wanted to go on, and now you demand we go on to see cows? Ki, this's cow country. It's poor but supportable, if enough is grazed, and we could've bumped across cows long before this. Now that you've convinced me to go back, it's not fair to insist we go on because you were serenaded by mooing ahigh!"

Jessie, wise to the range, stifled a smile. "Cattle are normally lazy bedders, Adele. Something set them off. We weren't hearing one or two peevish cows either, but a lengthy spell of herd-sized fuss. Not stampede-spooks from, say, a storm, but more like the sore afflictions we hear at branding time."

"Yes," Adele nodded, chagrined. "They've more smarts than I do."

Because of numerous rocky overhangs, it was particularly murky along the base of the canyon wall. Single-file, they walked their horses in that strip of gloom, slipping past the hut without incident and continuing on the trail as it skirted the sides of the bottle-neck canyon. Reaching the other end, they found that canyon mouth broadened into what the Mexicans call a *vallecito*, a pocket valley sprouting aspen, sage, and thick tufts of scratch-grass.

Mounting, they remained shadowed in the canyon mouth while carefully surveying the pocket valley and surrounding slopes. They tallied thirty steers loosely bunched in front of the canyon, and glimpsed countless more in similar gathers out about the valley floor, but spotted not a sign of any nighthawks or other hands camping out or riding herd. Warily, they started crossing the valley, full in the open for half a mile and sweating the entire distance, while they observed the cattle they happened to pass near. Many seemed to fidget while grazing or bedding down, and would stand twitchy or shamble aimlessly, making petulant noises. Judging by their condition, though, the herd consisted solely of choice beef described by Jessie as "plump juiciest prime." They all appeared to be carrying the Ledditt & Dinsmore LXD brand.

Pretty soon they reined in by a small brook trickling along a creased fold of bedrock. Stiff and exhausted, they knelt at the edge as their heaving, trembling horses sank their muzzles gratefully to the water and bordering grasses. Ki left them drinking to stroll toward some nearby cattle. As casual as he was, they stirred nervously at his approach, and required some soothing before he could inspect them at close range. Then he returned to his horse, and was uncoiling the frayed thirty-foot rope that'd been with the saddle gear, when Jessie and Adele came to ask what he'd found on those cattle.

"They've been recently branded, like we thought," he replied, patiently unkinking the rope. "LXD brand, with a heavy iron. The scorched hair odor is gone, but their hides still smart some and the burns haven't fully scabbed. I'd say that it'd been done around the time of the rustling, all right."

"Coincidence," Jessie sighed. "Like the coincidence that Pascal is one of the many working for LXD up Bridger Mountains way. Or so he says. Some sixty, eighty crow-flying miles away, and his railpoint would be Shoshone or Ocla, not Riverton. That's no coincidence; that's a link with Quinby."

"Here's another coincidence," Ki said, as he fashioned one rope end into a bowline for a lariat. "A not too commonly used cowtrail from the west, funneling off into here instead of going on to Riverton."

"I know. I'd hoped we'd've found worked-over Box M beef, but we haven't seen any brand-blotching or tampering, nothing except the LXD iron."

Adele nodded. "We must've tripped on a Ledditt & Dinsmore spread."

"And tangled our spurs," Jessie added sourly. "Ki? Where—"

Ki was asaddle, tying the other rope end to the horn. "Be ready to move fast if anyone takes notice of me," he called as he loped off, scanning the sweep of the valley. Spying no riders but remaining leery, he picked out a likely steer that was nosing around a thicket about forty yards away, and again wondered if he wasn't being a damn fool just because he'd felt his horse handled like it'd once been trained as a cow pony. The next few minutes could provide some potent revelations for everybody involved.

Swiftly Ki charged—or as swiftly as his pooped gelding could muster. Startled, the steer pivoted to run. The horse jerked, momentarily confused, then recovered, responding with ingrained habits by cutting and blocking the steer, allowing Ki to close in to spill his loop. Ki snagged the steer over the horns from behind, then flipped the rope to one side of the steer, while his horse veered to the other. The steer dropped, its hind legs wrenched out from under it. Ki lit down, and as the gelding held the catch-rope taut, he hog-tied the steer with half-rotted piggin strings.

Unsheathing his *tanto* knife, he crouched over the bawling, struggling steer and studied its flanks for iron brands. He found only one—another fresh LXD. Slicing around the brand, he peeled a ragged square of hide from the warm, meaty flesh as quickly, yet as gently, as possible. His field surgery was crude and not very humane, but the wound would eventually scar over, and his only alternative was to kill the steer. It was not his to kill; he wasn't sure precisely whose it was.

Ki released the steer, which scrambled upright, loud and mournful. Re-coiling his rope, he rode back to Jessie and Adele, and tried to ignore their questions while shaving off the hairs around the brand. At last he held the hide up against the pallid moonglow and, naturally, saw little through it.

But he saw enough. With a feral grin, he said, "Have a look."

Tight-lipped, Jessie regarded him for a moment, then took the hide from his outstretched hand. After studying it awhile, she noted, "Someone did a hasty job of branding, using too hot an iron that burned through at one point." She turned it this way and that some more, then passed the hide to Adele as she remarked to Ki, "What intrigues me most is what the brand conceals."

Adele extended it to the feeble light the way she had seen Jessie and Ki doing. "I see the LXD brand. So?"

"Anything else?"

"It's been burned on top of another brand. I still fail to—"

"What's the other brand?"

"I can't tell exactly, but I'm sure it's the same brand. Even *I* know rebranding is commonly done, for any number of reasons."

"A shame the LXD covers it over too well to read," Ki said affably, retrieving the hide and thrusting it into a vest pocket. "Maybe we'll be able to make it out clearer in good light."

They headed off again across the valley. On the far side they encountered another scrub-clogged canyon, which brought them to another section of broken and chopped roughlands, with yet another bench stretching beyond that. Without much in the way of moon or stars, it was impossible to gauge their direction accurately. But by keeping in a general line with the pocket canyon behind them and the Wind River buttes alongside them, they sensed they were heading easterly and would eventually come out close to Riverton. The paths took their own sweet time, however, and the horses were allowed to choose their own pace, which they maintained diligently without needing to be urged. As a result the riders unintentionally napped asaddle much of the way.

Gradually the land began to change, just as they had found it did on their initial leg of the trip. The crests grew smaller and more rounded, and the hollows shallower and dotted with brush. The horses seemed to champ at their bits, as if sensing the end of the journey.

There was a suspicious grayness, a false dawn, in the sky by the time they reached the main street of Riverton. Exhausted after another night's debauch, the tank town appeared shabby, drowsy—coasting while it caught its breath. The most noise echoed from the train yard, where by the sound of it, the longest freight ever assembled was being crashed together. The places that had been the noisest, the saloons and card mills, were open but barely functioning. Virtually everyplace else was shuttered and locked, dead to the world.

The livery was closed. Despite that, and despite their own needs, the three riders figured the welfare of their mounts came first. They rousted the grizzled old sot of a hostler, who was sleeping off a toot in the stable hay crib, and he threw a conniption fit until Jessie offered twenty bucks for one day's grooming and graining for their animals. She also tried to rent fresh horses to use in the meantime, but the hostler was plumb sorry, his every last plug had been rented by town possemen out hunting a coupla killers.

Using that as his cue, Ki declared genially, "I'm sure your sheriff is very proud of such citizen support. I assume he's out leading the chase?"

"Doubtful. His horse is here." The hostler thumbed at a stall holding a blaze-faced Trigueño. "Got a cracked foreshoe. The horse, I mean."

"The sheriff's right; his duty is to stay and patrol the town."

"True, but he wouldn't be now. He gen'rally retires at two ayem."

"A man to learn from," Jessie stated. "There any restaurant open?"

"The Express Café, a block from the depot, to your left."

"Much obliged."

They stepped back up the street, following the hostler's directions. The Express proved to be an all-night railroader's café, and its food proved to be a good/bad—news proposition, the bad news being it was terrible, the good news being there was plenty of it. They ate greedily, and despite the unpalatable cooking, they left the café feeling immeasurably refreshed.

They angled toward the Continental Hotel.

Jessie glanced at Adele and worried. From practically the moment they'd met, Adele had been facing peril, cheating death; and Jessie didn't want to endanger her further. Yet here they were heading into the worst threat yet. Quinby's actions last night, his schemes to kill her, whatever his motive, proved he was a butcher—vicious, unscrupulous, one to be handled with a measure of care. A method should be figured, if possible, to blunt Quinby's fangs themselves rather than to trust the job to fate. How to do it? No answer had come to her along the ride here, and no immediate solution occurred to her now as she approached the hotel entrance.

They entered softly, pausing just inside the doors. Customers were still drinking in the club bar, while tired dance-hall girls sat around or helped the bartenders cleaning up the mess. The lobby was deserted except for the desk clerk, who sat tilted back in a chair, his feet propped on a stool. He had dozed off while reading a popular pink-paper weekly.

Despite his face being sunk in the paper, the clerk was recognizable to Ki. "Melvin," he said disgustedly. "Jessie, do you know Quinby's room?"

"No. He mentioned he lives here, that's all. Thank heavens you had the brains to pump that hostler, or I wouldn't even know Quinby was here now."

Adele suggested, "Let's go check the register and pigeonholes."

"If Melvin woke, he'd identify us and scream bloody murder."

"Then I'll do it, Ki." Smiling, Adele started forward.

Jessie gasped. "No, please don't try."

Adele already was trying. She ignored Jessie. She glided over to the desk, and, while Melvin snored lustily into his paper, she ferreted around him. She found the register under Melvin's feet on the stool, and Jessie and Ki tensed, breathless, as Adele calmly lifted Melvin's legs, removed the book, leafed through it and stuck it back under the clerk. She eased onto the stairs, motioning for them to join her.

With a kind of grudging haste, Jessie hurried a pace behind Ki.

"Sneaky does it," Adele said. "Sheriff Quinby is in Twenty-one."

Ki's eyes narrowed. "That's next to Slats Burdou's room . . ."

No one in the barroom paid them any attention as they mounted the rickety staircase. The corridor was empty at the moment, foul-smelling as before, a din of snoring filtering from behind closed doors as they walked along the hall to room 21. They paused just outside Quinby's door. Immediately to the left was the room where someone had stabbed the Box M foreman to death and stolen his information. To the right hung one of the hall's few low-burning bracket lamps, and a fair stretch beyond that was the front stairs landing.

Jessie whispered to Adele, "You should stay out here."

Adele did not reply. She just looked at Jessie.

"You should; to watch the stairs and for guests coming out rooms."

"No use, Jessie. I'm as adamant as you. Besides, if you want to convince my father of anything, you need me in there to tell him what I've witnessed."

Jessie hesitated, still reluctant to get Adele involved, then acquiesced, nodding as she drew her pistol. Ki smothered a grin, thinking Jessie now knew how she herself was to deal with, as he noiselessly palmed the doorknob to Quinby's room. Then almost as an afterthought, he eyed Adele gravely and said, "Don't say a word. No names, no questions, nothing, no matter what."

"Agreed. You can tell me what to do, except to go."

The door was locked, but the flimsy catch broke readily under Ki's battering shoulder. He and Jessie darted swiftly into the room with Adele a step behind, as they wheeled to cover the man sprawled on top of the blanketed bed there, clad in undershirt and cotton drawers. It was Sheriff Quinby, deep in slumber. The lawman's shell-belt hung from a peg on the window frame. His boots, pants, and shirt were scattered in disarray on the floor. Dead to the world, Quinby had not stirred yet.

Ki appropriated Quinby's revolver and handed it to Adele. He drew down the window shade while Jessie lighted a coal-oil lamp on the bureau.

Sheriff Quinby strangled on a snore and sat bolt upright as he felt the cold kiss of a pistol prodding his cheek. Automatically he yawned, the yawn choking off as it dawned on him that he was staring into the bore of a Colt.

"Don't make a sound, Sheriff," Jessie whispered.

"We're going to have a little confab before breakfast, and you'll be a dead man if you make a single false move."

Quinby's eyes lost their sleepy gaze and a yellow glint of horror took its place. He snapped a glance at the closed door, then at his empty holster hanging from the window frame. "Yuh—yuh can't get away with this, yuh dumb slut!" he snarled, swinging his sock-clad feet over the edge of the bed. Beneath his underwear, his chest was heaving violently. "The whole town, the whole reservation knows you're wanted for murder!"

"Give me any trouble, and that charge will be true," Jessie retorted in a voice that could jelly marrow. She drew up the room's only chair and sat down, holstering her pistol. Across the room, Adele leaned against the door, the sheriff's revolver gripped at the ready. Ki peered out the side of the window blind, then came over and stood beside Jessie, one hand on the back rung of her chair.

"Let's start easy," Jessie said. "Why'd you kill Slats Burdou?"

"You can't prove such wild talk! You're shootin' in the dark."

Jessie glanced up at Ki. "Lend me your knife. I think the time has come to do some fancy throat-whittling."

Sheriff Quinby smirked, obviously convinced that Jessie was pretending. Adele didn't look too sure, but didn't look like she'd care for the consequences of it either way. Ki knew full well that Jessie was bluffing; that she was constitutionally incapable of cold-blooded torture; and that whether she tried to play out the bluff and force herself actually to do it, the result could be the sheriff wresting the upper hand from her. And Quinby would not hesitate to indulge in his threats. That left it up to Ki, who found strong-arm tactics repugnant but knew how to use them efficiently and effectively. He gave Jessie an imperceptible shake of the head, as

Quinby laced his hands over a drawn-up knee and declared defiantly, "I dunno a damn thing, and if I did, I wouldn't tell you!"

Ki sprang at Quinby before Quinby finished his sentence. His right arm hooked around Quinby's neck and he pulled back, driving the hard bone of his forearm into the sheriff's throat while he dumped him off the cot onto his knees. In the process, Ki's left arm went under Quinby's armpit and his left hand behind the sheriff's neck, pushing hard against the right side of his head. The choke was complete.

"Better than a knife. No telltale blood, no loud cries," Ki told Jessie, pulling back against Quinby's throat with his right forearm, and pushing forward on the head with his right hand.

"Awwwk!" Quinby made a dry, ugly sound like a sick bird, his face turning red, his eyes bulging, both hands clutching Ki's rock-hard forearm. Ki held it almost too long, almost, then relaxed a smidgen. "Air . . . Couldn't breathe . . ." Quinby panted in a hoarse whisper. "T-talk, anything yuh . . . want!"

"That's better," Jessie snapped. "Why'd you kill Slats Burdou?"

"L-listen, I didn't." Quinby's tongue was out, his head turned sideways. Still on his knees, he continued to make that ugly sound. "N-not me."

"Was it Oscar Pascal's doing?"

Quinby nodded, trembling. "Okay, yeah . . . yeah . . ."

"Why did Pascal kill Burdou?"

"Pascal found out that Burdou wasn't jus' a grubline waddie, a harmless coot, like he made out to be. He found out Burdou was Box M foreman, tryin' to get the deadwood on what happened to that shipment. O-only one what was; only one sniffin' the right track. Pascal feared he'd found out something."

"What?"

"I dunno."

Ki pulled his forearm back, cutting into Quinby's windpipe, pushing the head forward at the same time with his left hand. Quinby's mouth was open as he tried to speak, but no sound came out until Ki finally relaxed his hold.

"I . . . I don't know," Quinby wheezed. "I don't, honest . . ."

"Where is Pascal now?"

"I dunno where; I don't work for him."

"What are you, partners? Go on, Quinby. Don't get ignorant on us now. Tell us everything you know about Pascal."

"L-listen! Y'know the kinda setup I got cookin' here; yuh gotta believe Pascal ain't the only guy I'm dealing with. What's there to know? I sell him some blindeye, make sure his men don't get in no problems hereabouts, grease things along. That's why Pascal does his shippin' outta here instead o' Ocla."

Jessie eyed him disdainfully. "There's more to it than that."

"No, I—" Quinby stiffened, straightening up, feeling an iron collar of pain around his neck. "Aw'ri'! Aw'ri'! When Pascal was in prison, I helped get members of his owlhoot bunch enlisted and stationed at Fort Washakie. I know the noncoms and j.g.'s out there, and sometimes they need favors, so sometimes I need favors. A-and when Pascal got out, I vouched for him, made him a deputy, pufferied him up so he'd land a job with one of the Ledditt and Dinsmore subsidiary spreads."

"Why?"

"The syndicate isn't always handled on very tight lines, as you know. Pascal has leased LXD range up toward Billings, Montana, and his job has been to stock that range with cattle to sell under the LXD brand."

"Why, Pascal sounds like a fine homebody. Setting up his own ranch, and running a lot of rustled stock through under a trusted, captive brand. Keep talking, Quinby," Jessie snapped. "You're not out of the woods yet by a heck of a long sight."

"That—that's all I know." Quinby moaned despondently as Ki applied more pressure. "It is! I swear, it's the gospel truth!"

Jessie rose, setting the chair aside. Ki took it as a signal that she was finished, and eased the pressure on Quinby's throat. The half-conscious sheriff, now a bright red, struggled to get to his feet, still clutching Ki's forearm. Then Jessie turned and faced Quinby again, pondering a new thought.

"Getting back to Slats, Quinby. Who knifed him?"

"Three of his men are takin' credit so far, but my feelin' is that Pascal did him in himself. So's not to take any chances on foul-ups." Air was coming to Quinby in thimblefuls; his lungs burned and his throat was one dull ache. "I was takin' a nap in here when I heard someone snoopin' around Burdou's room. That's when I busted in and arrested you." Quinby was half on his feet, body in a sitting position but without a chair under him, and that's when Jessie gave Ki a slight nod, and Ki chopped Quinby lightly underneath the jawbone. A stupid look slid over Quinby's face and he sagged to the floor.

"We've wrung enough out of Quinby for right now," Jessie said. "I think what needs to be done next is for you, Ki, to go tell Major Thinnes the situation, and bring him back to hear the sheriff's story."

Ki frowned. "No, I don't like leaving you with Quinby."

"One of us must go. And Quinby won't be any trouble; we'll use his handcuffs to lock him to the bedstead."

Adele now spoke up. "Look, I can ride alone to the fort."

"I don't like that idea any better," Ki responded. "Pascal's gunmen are still out hunting us. And two can prevail on the major better than one."

"Oh, I'll give Dad an earful. When I'm done, he'll not only send a squad here for you, but he'll send a platoon or more to the mine to root out Pascal's gang."

"That might not be for the best, Adele," Jessie cautioned. "First we should find out if a trooper nicknamed Reno is on the fort's muster roll and, if so, if he's on active duty or absent without leave. And we should check on who Reno palled around with. Otherwise, if there're rustlers among the troops, they could forewarn Pascal and they'd all escape, or even trap the platoon in an ambush." She rubbed her forehead, trying to clear her fatigued mind, then took her hotel room key out of her pocket and handed it to Ki. "It might be wise to pick up our gear on the way out. It could get awkward later."

"I still don't like it much," Ki said, acquiescing. "You keep sharp guard, Jessie. If Quinby makes a false move, blast him to pieces."

"With great pleasure. I've a hunch he killed Burdou, and not Pascal, like he wants us to believe."

After cuffing the unconscious sheriff to the iron frame of his bed, Ki and Adele stepped to the door, glanced both ways along the corridor, and departed. Jessie closed the door, though its broken latch prevented her from locking it securely, and sat down to await Ki's return with Major Thinnes.

Presently came the dawn. As the early morning sun rose, so did the guests in the hotel. The sounds of doors and bootfalls echoed along the corridor. Gradually the town outside stirred awake, and about the time daylight outside was glowing brassily through the window shade, Sheriff Quinby stirred awake, too.

They eyed each other in silence for quite some while longer.

"Miz Starbuck," Quinby said suddenly, licking his lips tentatively, "you look like a smart lady to me."

"Smart enough to shoot you dead."

Quinby made a sickly attempt at a grin. He gestured, straining on the cuffs, toward the bureau where the lamp was burning. "Miz Starbuck, look. I've got a handbox yonder with a thousand dollars in gold. It's—"

Jessie laughed caustically. "Blood money, Sheriff? The loot Pascal paid you to kill Slats Burdou, or what you'd have paid Gabriel to kill me?"

Quinby started to rise, but the handcuffs and Jessie's leveled pistol caused him to sit back down again abruptly. "Poker winnin's, I swear. Look, I'm only a tool. I got no part in Pascal's fancy doin's. That thousand is all yours, li'l lady, if yuh just let me have the cuff key, drag my clothes on and light a shuck outta Riverton."

"Not for a million, Quinby. You're going to pay, but not in money."

Footsteps sounded out in the hall, stopping at the sheriff's room. Someone tapped on the door, followed by a jingling of keys.

"Who's there?" Jessie called.

A rather bored woman's voice answered, "The maid. I got towels."

Jessie padded to the door, still covering Quinby. She pressed her ear to the wood and listened intently, but didn't catch anything suspicious; no heavy creaking of boots or low breathing of men waiting beside the maid. If she refused to let the maid in, it might look suspicious and cause the clerk to come check. If she allowed the maid in, though . . .

"Sit there and put a cover over those cuffs," she ordered to Quinby. "One move, one peep to the maid and you'll get it. Whatever else, you'll die."

"Sure, sure. I tell yuh, yuh got me all wrong."

Jessie swung open the door and stepped back, shielding her pistol from casual view. A brown-haired, full-figured woman in a tight maid's outfit entered with a stack of towels. She smiled vaguely at Jessie and then at the sheriff, saying only, "Sorry t' disturb you. I'll make it snappy." She went to the washstand and began replacing the rack of towels, humming to herself.

"Never mind changing the sheets, neither," Quinby said to her, the cuff chain rattling a little as he shifted his position.

Jessie kept her eye trained on him. In his desperate straits, she could believe him capable of anything if not watched like a hawk. As a result, she failed to see that along with the dirty towels, the maid swept up the water pitcher. She failed to see her blank expression change to one of mean determination, and her two swift, silent strides to the chair, the pitcher high over her head.

All Jessie knew was an abrupt, blinding explosion inside her brain as the hard ceramic water pitcher collided with her skull. Blackness surged in, but she fought against it as, without realizing, she slumped floorward.

Dimly she heard Quinby shout, "Good work, Delores! Now, get the key to these cuffs off'n her. Hurry!"

Hastily the maid fumbled at Jessie's clothing. "Yeah, I am. I figured I owed you this one, to make up for me not milkin' any info outta her partner."

"Him! This bitch won't be seein' Ki this side of Hades!"

Then something like a sledgehammer struck her temple, and Jessie plunged into a black vortex where she knew no pain, no fear—only crushing darkness.

Chapter 9

Earlier, while dawn was yet a promise in the east and tepid air hung motionless over slumbering Riverton, Ki and Adele sneaked out the rear of the hotel and returned to the livery stable. The hostler, irascible at being awakened again so soon, warned they'd get no refund for picking up their cayuses early. Ki thanked him anyway and packed his and Jessie's bags on the scarcely rested horses. Then they rode out of town.

The wagon road south, like the railroad, crossed the Wind River at the town limits. The cable ferry there, however, had a number of tough hombres hanging around its docking ramp, so Adele and Ki jogged west awhile, searching for a less risky spot to ford.

Overland through a short range of rough breaks, piney slopes and brushy draws they rode, out of sight as much as possible, continuously wary for sight or sound of other riders. Speed was impossible. They would walk their mounts, then prod them into a brisk lope for a while, never faster; and at intervals they would pause for short rests, for the horses simply had no more bottom left. Sometimes, though, the cavalry pony that Adele rode would dance sideways, bumping shoulders with Ki's gelding. After the first couple of times, Ki grew aware that Adele's knee would nudge his thigh, and that she would lean near with her hands locked on the saddlehorn, faintly smiling in a tantalizing manner. And he began to get the idea that she was getting ideas.

Pale streaks of light were slashing through the

brightened eastern sky when the animal path they happened to be following veered down into a gorge. The gorge was steeply sloped, hopper-shaped, overgrown with broad-leaved cottonwood and box-elder trees, with the bed of the Wind River serving as its floor. Ki recalled the cattle-trail ford was calmer and not as compressed between sheer walls. Still, here was a far cry from the normally rampaging cascades, though its swirling flow was quite enough to make any sensible rider apprehensive and very careful.

"It's likely as good as we're going to find," he judged.

"I won't fall in, don't worry." Adele smiled, but went on speaking, as if she had not paused again to sidle against him. "But then, I imagine you aren't much for worrying. You take things as they come, as they are."

Ki could have kissed her, sensing Adele wanted to learn what his mouth might be like on her lips. But he merely grinned and urged his horse down the incline, and saw the frown that came and went so suddenly on her face, like a dark storm cloud scudding before a warm chinook. Apparently the major's daughter was not one to be trifled with, especially when she hankered to do some trifling of her own.

Cautiously, they waded into the chilly flow. The horses struggled across, hoofs fighting for purchase on the slippery, sharp rocks, legs resisting the buffeting of the current. Finally, lurching, all but falling, they pawed up the bank toward the screened, wooded ridge on the south side of the gorge. After a steadying breath atop the ridge, they loped into the brush immediately ahead.

They were rounding a patch of Doonhead thistle when a voice said behind them, "Well, now, jus' where d'you reckon you're goin'?"

They reined in, careful to keep straight and quiet until they faced the voice. They saw, astride a bay, a swarthy man in dirt-crusted garb, curly black hair peeking out from the open neck of his shirt and from beneath his sweat-stained hat. He had spoken pleasantly enough, but his eyes were as hard as bottler glass, and his right thumb was hooked in his sagging gunbelt, an inch or so above the butt of a .45.

"Merely passing through," Ki answered genially. "We must've gotten lost a dozen times so far. Hard on my wife, her in the family way and all."

The man looked annoyed. "Let's get it done."

Two more men suddenly dove from the surrounding bush. They'd been sneaking around in a flanking attack, that much was obvious to Ki—just as obvious as the motives of the swarthy man who, seeing his opportunity, drew his revolver while charging directly at Adele.

The other two men landed in front of and beside Ki, swiveling to fire. The one in front shot. Ki flicked a *shuriken* star-blade a split second sooner. The thistle patch resounded with the revolver's report, the man's bullet spanging off a sunbaked rock. Then he sank rolling on the ground, choking and gasping, a star-shaped disk protruding from his throat.

The second man stared disbelievingly, then blinked as flashes of metal whizzed through the air before his eyes. A *shuriken* slashed high into his abdomen, and another, better placed, sliced like a scalpel between his ribs and imbedded itself in the man's heart. He collapsed atop his throat-slit pal.

"Fuck!" the swarthy man snarled, struggling to get in an accurate shot with his pistol while shielding himself with Adele's twisting body. "Hold it!" he warned, dragging her closer to him, up out of her saddle. "You try'n snicker-snee me, buddy, an' the bitch earns it!"

Helpless, Ki watched the swarthy man as he jabbed the muzzle of his pistol into the nape of her neck. Adele was still writhing frantically, her mouth widening to scream. The man rashly clamped a hand over her face, and she bit his palm. Now it was the man who screamed, letting go.

Immediately, Adele plunged headlong to the ground. The man fired. Ki felt the bullet rip along his right arm, shredding the sleeve of his shirt as he let loose another *shuriken*. There was an explosive grunt as the man toppled backward from his saddle, the *shuriken* buried in his upper left pectorals. Using his horse for cover, he sprinted into the thin but rugged strip of boulders and trees that bordered the ridge.

"Stay flat!" Ki ordered Adele, launching down after the man. He saw a gun barrel poke around the peak of a boulder, and with an abrupt surge to the left, he dove behind a fallen pine tree just as a gunshot gouged splinters overhead. The shot placed the man for him. He began inching noiselessly through the rocks and brush toward that position.

'You shit!" the man yelled. "You goddam shit!" He fired again, furrowing a second white gash of bare wood through the darker bark of the pine.

Ki paused, gauging by the voice and shot that the man was retreating softly toward the edge of the gorge. There were only a few yards separating him and the man, but they consisted of a thick fence of briars, boulders, and trees. No open space for pitching *shuriken* blades or his throwing daggers. He continued to ease nearer, quietly unsheathing his belt knife—his short, curve-bladed *tanto*. It was deadly in hand-to-hand combat and was his best choice now.

"I'll kill you! You 'n' the cunt, y'hear?"

Ki leaped toward the voice, a steely grin etched on his face as he bounded from boulder to boulder across the uneven ground. He could hear a shuffling in the underbrush ahead as the man swiveled to bring his revolver to bear. He pivoted off the slope of a rock, sighting the man by the rim. The man was bleeding, wheezing, but he had a lethal glint to his eyes, a firmness to his stance, as he trained his revolver. Ki scarcely had an instant's grace to dart aside before the revolver lanced flame and lead ricocheted off the rocks next to him in a shower of sparks.

Instantly, Ki lunged forward, slashing underhanded with his knife. The blade bit into the man's belly, and Ki sliced upward through his brisket as though gutting an animal. Warm blood gushed over the hilt and his hand. The man teetered away, off the blade, and spun over the edge in a long fall to the gorge below. Ki peered down from the ridge at the splayed body, face down in the river, rocking gently from the current roiling around it. Then he turned and wearily started back.

He met Adele on the way. She had followed him as far as a small mossy spot near the fallen pine tree, and was standing hunched with head lowered, both hands on her knees.

"It's over," Ki said gently, patting her shoulder.

She shook her head in disgust at her own behavior. Her color grew better, and she decided she wasn't going to be sick. "I'm sorry. It's silly of me, but it got to my nerves. They wanted to kill us."

"Pascal wanted to kill us. They were just obeying orders."

She snuggled closer. "And I said I could ride alone," she whispered contritely. A shiver rippled through her. Ki conjured up things to say that might comfort her, but she kissed him before he could open his mouth.

It was an affectionate kiss at first, lazy and teasing. Then it changed, and a smoldering passion seemed to take fire in her. She pressed against him, squirming and rubbing, her mouth like a bitter fruit that would give a man pain when he tasted it.

Ki knew she was scared and dejected and in need of the support he could give her. But he wasn't sure she needed to be given the support that was hardening in response to her torrid kiss—not here, anyway, not yet. So after a moment of tight-locking lips, he drew back and said reluctantly, "Let's go."

She tilted her head. "Is it Jessie? Is it some other woman?"

"Not Jessie, no; and not any woman."

"Well, if no woman's got you by the chandeliers, Ki, why're you balking at my offer?" She nuzzled his chest, her eyes mocking. "I owe you. I've only one thing of value, so I'm paying. With interest."

"Great. I'll collect later."

"The debt is due now." With open mouth and slowly sliding tongue, she kissed him again, lazily, sensuously. "I'm not a society belle virgin, all coyness and honey," she murmured. "I'm a widow, twice over—my husbands both officers killed in Indian combat. Short lived, short loved, and I decided when I returned home and resumed my maiden name to go after what I felt like having when I feel like having it. And I willingly admit it."

"Bluntly, too."

"If there's anything frontier military life does, it strips away the nonessentials." And with that, Adele stripped off her clothes. Humming provocatively, she pulled her shirt over her head, letting it float to the moss. Her pants went next, down to her knees. Her firm plump breasts swayed gracefully as she sat down and drew off each pantleg and boot. Naked save for her drawers, she grabbed for Ki'd denims. "What's keeping you?"

Ki felt that tug all the way through his taut loins. He needed Adele like he needed a bad case of poison ivy, but he supposed that was what made men different from women. When a woman was wanting, a man will somehow rise to the occasion. Besides, the horses needed a brief respite.

He reached for her and got a handful of thin white cotton. Drawers off and gone, Adele crushed her body to his, kissing with hot, moist urgency. She helped him out of his clothes, then pushed him slowly down, kissing his neck and ears, until he was lying on his back. Then, working lower, hot and moist, she laved his chest and stomach, teased his navel, and dipped to the insides of his thighs. She kissed him wetly there, let her tongue drag on his skin, and then when the tension was unbearable, she went down on him open-mouthed, wide, hot, trying to swallow all of his girth. She slid her hands under his hips and encouraged his movements, giving with his upward thrusts, taking as much as she could. The roof of her mouth was ridged and hard, and her soft palate behind the hardness was a tantalizing thrill. Her tongue was rough, teasing his sensitivity. Then she went the length of him, down until her nose was against his groin, and back his entire length to repeat, and repeat again.

Ki could feel a tumultuous eruption building, building in his scrotum. Too soon, he thought, too soon . . . Forcing himself to break free, he twisted up and around, planting his knees between her squirming thighs, feeling her ready and moist with yearning anticipation.

Reaching between them, Adele grasped his turgid shaft with one hand, using her other hand to fondle her pubes and spread them for his entry. Ki sank forward, entering her with her guidance, feeling her grip around his entire length with a firmness that almost drove him crazy. Adele sang out her delight, her arms wrapping tightly around his back, pulling him down against her breasts, her body following his rhythm in wild abandonment. Her nails began digging spasmodically, slithering down to claw at the flesh of his pumping buttocks, thrusting him deeper into her while her thighs splayed wide on the moss beneath her.

Satisfying Adele's ravenous needs was exhausting. Snaking his tongue inside her mouth, Ki hoped to calm her briefly and regain his strength. It was a futile attempt. More frenziedly now, she locked her ankles firmly around him, her nude flesh slippery from the sweat of her burgeoning passion. Arching her buttocks, she humped up and down, undulating slowly at first, then faster, faster—until finally every sensation surging within their bodies was expelled, and they collapsed, satiated . . .

She chuckled contentedly. "How's that for my pay-back?"

"In full," Ki said, mustering the energy to ease out of her. He tottered upright and groped for his clothes. "Come on, we've got to get a move on."

Yawning and stretching, Adele rose to her feet. Ki, dressed, walked on to the horses, checked their rigging and tightened the straps, then dragged the first two dead men into the bushes. If Pascal checked on them, he'd rather it wasn't learned too quickly that the hunters were dead and, by inference, that the hunted had gotten past and were on ahead.

Adele arrived, looking fresh and eager for more. Re-mounting, she leaned across to give Ki a peck on the cheek. Then they set off, blazing a fresh trail on what he hoped was a direct route to the Fort Washakie wagon road.

The sky turned from pearl gray to slate blue, and was beginning to flush with a warmer color when Ki noticed a high knoll that looked vaguely familiar. Veering to-ward it, they struck an angular shelf that he knew he'd seen before. Then they intersected the road he recog-nized as the one which led from Arapaho to Fort Washakie.

Through habitual alertness, Ki scanned the roadway in either direction, but there was no sign of Pascal's killers having traced them to this juncture. The rest of their journey was ridden at as swift a pace as the flag-ging horses could maintain.

Eventually, under a nooning sun, they pushed up that final long grade to the military post and went straight to the headquarters building. There, a patently enamoured Lieutenant Pomfrit blushed and stammered his way through telling Adele that her father had just left for lunch at their house. Thanking him, they remounted and rode across the company area toward Officers' Row.

"Let's skirt around," Ki advised, when he spotted Sergeant Neville marching a squad toward the railway yard. Yonder there he glimpsed the Forney 4-4-T locomotive taking on water at the tanks. Behind the squat tender was a flatcar loaded with another detail of troopers from, Ki surmised, Neville's Third Platoon of F company.

Taking a long detour around, they came in from the opposite end of Officers' Row and reined in by the whitewashed house. The sentry on duty jumped to attention and saluted as they stepped to the porch, although technically they didn't rate a salute. The rank of commandant's daughter, however, had persuasive influence. Entering, they heard the gruff voices of Major Thinnes and Hep Mulhollan rumbling from the dining room, and when they went in, the men almost choked on their food as they stopped talking and stood up.

"Great Caesar's ghost!" the major blurted. "Where've you been, Adele? You look like you were caught in a cave-in!"

"Almost," Adele replied, giving him a kiss on the cheek. Then she nodded warmly at Mulhollan and, with a sigh, settled into a chair. The housekeeper came in, gasped "Lawdy!" and waddled out proclaiming a hot meal was a sure remedy. By then the men had all sat down. Ki and Adele began relating their experiences—except for some judicious editing of more personal incidents that had occurred. Thinnes expressed shock at the news of Sheriff Quinby's duplicity, while Mulhollan grew excited over the pocket valley where the LXD-branded herd was discovered.

The frowning Box M boss stated, "That don't sound big 'nuff for no reg'lar ranch operation, but an awful much like a cattle cache."

"A what?" Adele asked.

"A stopover for herds bein' driven from one point to

another," he explained. "But y'found no other sign? No Box M stuff? I mean, considerin' how long you've been gone and what you've run into, was that all?"

The major sputtered, "Look at Adele, Hep! Wasn't that enough?"

"My cows!"

"My daughter!"

"My word!" Adele gasped.

"My God!" Ki snapped, and banged the table with his fist, quieting the outbursts. He removed the hide from his pocket then, and passed it around. "No, that was not all. The LXD brand's a burn-over, concealing another."

The two men, and Adele for a second time, inspected the hide by the better light of the room's lamps. They each made the discovery that Ki had been hoping for, that he and Jessie discerned dimly back at the valley. Part of the brand was horny scar tissue, traceable as the army's U.S. iron. But a hot running iron had made the U into a larger L, and had turned the S into partly an X and partly the round bottom of a lower case d, creating the distinctive brand of the Ledditt & Dinsmore beef syndicate.

"What about the underbit and crop earmarks?" Mulhollan asked Ki.

"Different. Larger, large enough to have vented the Box M's; and I bet they're registered to some spread that Pascal has a hand in running." Ki gazed sternly about the table. "Earmarks or not, you know what it means when a brand is worked over like this one was. The herd was rustled."

Thinnes brooded thoughtfully as he lit a cigar. "On the basis of what's here, well . . . I'm inclined to believe the Box M had nothing to do with the shipment of cull stuff. Pardon me." He arose and stalked out. The front door opened, and after a moment it shut and the major returned to sit down and resume his conversation. "I also tend to agree with Miss Starbuck about checking the troops before trusting them. Trooper Alperson outside recollects that the cavalryman nicknamed Reno deserted six months ago from Sergeant Neville's platoon."

"Neville!" Mulhollan bellowed. "Ain't he the bluebelly you put in charge of my first shipment, and, just this morning, in charge of my second shipment?"

Thinnes nodded, explaining to Ki and Adele, "Word came there's a trainload of Box M beef due at Riverton late tonight, and naturally I assigned the Third Platoon to transfer it here safely." Thinnes eyed Mulhollan again, adding, "Calm down, Hep. I'll have the scoundrels, including Sheriff Quinby, clapped in irons by time your replacement beef arrives in Riverton."

"Wal, time's a-wastin'! Pascal will drove the cached herd right quick, and there'll go the proof to clear me and pinch him. C'mon, let's get to doin' like Miz Jessie wants an' needs, an' go relieve her of one bent badge-toter."

"You? You can't go. You're a prisoner."

Mulhollan leaned toward Thinnes, jaw jutting. "Try'n stop me."

"You cantankerous ol' curmudgeon! I've an entire army I can—"

"Why you braid-brained, officious pri—"

"Mister Mulhollan!" Adele gasped.

"Prig," Mulhollan finished, snatching the major's cigar out of his mouth and grinding it out in the ashtray. "I'm in your custody, I am, and I'll go with you to round up my own affairs if'n I hafta boot you the entire way!"

"We could use a gun we can count on," Ki suggested to Thinnes.

Thinnes was spluttering, his face reddening. "Oh . . . Very well. I'll requisition mounts, including a fresh one for you, Ki, and we'll shove off."

"And just what am I supposed to do in the meanwhile?" Adele demanded. "Sit in my room?"

The major made the mistake of saying, "Sounds reasonable to me. You must be tired after your ordeal, and this won't be woman's work, m'dear, and—"

"And nothing doing," she cut in tersely. "I'm going too, whether along with you guys or close behind."

Major Thinnes looked at her, fidgeted, and shrugged. "Better off with us, if you insist, where at least we can shelter you some." He glanced woefully at Mulhollan, complaining, "I swan, she's more obstinate than her mother, who hailed from Missouri." And then he and Mulhollan both sighed the sigh of men plagued by women.

After lunch, Ki and Adele turned in their exhausted horses for a pair of hard-muscled geldings that looked enough alike to be foal brothers. Major Thinnes chose the same mount he'd ridden yesterday, a parade-glossy black. Hep Mulhollan reclaimed his moleskin grulla and high-cantle stock rig, along with a holstered plow-handle Colt and a .50 Sharps which he lugged in a custom saddle boot.

With a minimum of flurry, they left the fort. Through early afternoon, cantering hoofbeats lifted tawny dust along the wagon road to Arapaho—a scruffy settlement, Ki discovered, which displayed all the earmarks of a lusty and tough trade—and from there northeastward to Riverton. Travel by road rather than cross-country allowed them to sustain a steady gait that covered the miles quicker without overtaxing their horses. Not until they reached the Wind River did they slow appreciably, approaching the cable ferry warily, on the lookout for Pascal's gunmen or other suspicious characters.

Yet none were to be seen, either on the ferry or at the docking ramps. That was a relief to Adele, but Ki couldn't help wondering why the men they'd spotted that morning had withdrawn, and as they entered Riverton, he kept his senses attuned to anything out of the ordinary, any detail that might indicate some surprise ahead. The town, however, appeared bored and logy. Most of the locals had run their errands by now, and most of the outlying ranchers couldn't be expected to arrive much before late afternoon. A couple of drunks were staggering down the main street. A gaggle of bonneted women were gossiping in the shade of the mercantile store. The bootmaker's dog was snapping at flies. Proprietors lounged in shop doorways, waiting out the dull afternoon for the surge of evening business.

Reining in by the Continental Hotel, they walked into the lobby and saw that the rat-faced clerk, Melvin, had been replaced by a thin, bespectacled clerk, to whom they nodded perfunctorily as they went upstairs. Reaching the landing, they strode down the corridor to Quinby's room.

"You may object to the tactics I'll have to use to oil the sheriff's voice," Ki said, knocking on the door. "But it might be necessary."

"I don't care a hoot," Mulholaln responded, "if you blow his head off."

"Jessie?" Ki knocked again, but there was still no response. *"Jessie!"* He shoved against the broken lock, opening the door. Sunlight glowing through the window shade revealed a disheveled bed and the lamp still burning on the bureau, but no trace of Jessie or Sheriff Quinby.

"They can't have gone!" Adele gasped, staring around.

Major Thinnes scowled. "Then where are they?"

"Nothin' to get your dander up about," Mulhollan said. "Miz Jessie probably had to move Quinby before someone came looking for him."

Ki might have accepted that explanation if he hadn't caught sight of a smear of coagulating blood on the floor near the threshold. "No—something's happened to her," he replied grimly. "I doubt Quinby broke loose and overwhelmed Jessie on his own. More likely, I fear, some plug-ugly in his pay must have discovered we were badgering the sheriff in his den, and rescued him after we left her here by herself."

Adele paled. "In that case . . ."

"Yes—Jessie might be dying or dead, dumped anyplace," Ki finished, despair laying its acid taste on his tongue. "Come on, we must find her!"

They left the room, Adele closing the door behind them. Returning to the lobby, they asked the desk clerk if he'd noticed the sheriff or a woman answering Jessie's description go out.

"Nope," he answered. "I ain't seen no traffic since I came on duty. It's been quieter'n a prairie dog's burrow."

"When did you come on duty?" Adele demanded.

"Ten ayem, earlier'n usual, on account the clerk before me was gone."

"Melvin?" Ki impetuously leaned across the counter and grasped the clerk by his shirtfront. "Where'd Melvin go?"

"I dunno! Not home, that was tried. I reckon out drinking, him'n that maid he's sweet on; they both thirst after the sauce, but I dunno for sure. H-how could I? They'd vamoosed when I was called in, okay?"

"Okay," Ki growled, thrusting the clerk away.

The rest of the time in Riverton was a nightmare to Ki. From the hotel he led them hurriedly to the train yard, hoping Quinby had imprisoned Jessie in the stockade car again. The jail on wheels was back in its old position on the spur, its side door padlocked, neither light nor sound coming from within. They did see, however, that Box M's cattle train had arrived from Natrona. It was shunted off the main line onto the army's siding, where it awaited the engine and detail from Fort Washakie.

"Odd," Major Thinnes commented, watching. "I was

told the C&NW wouldn't pull in until late tonight, perhaps even tomorrow morning."

"Who told you?"

"Why, a trooper from Sergeant Neville's platoon reported the news."

"Then there's nothing odd about it," Mulhollan said darkly.

Upon Adele's suggestion, they split up to search the town proper systematically. Ki went to the livery stable and learned from the hostler that Quinby had fetched his Trigueño and Jessie's mare along about nine that morning, giving no reason, but acting in a frothing hurry.

Ki then hastened to the rear of the hotel, where he hunkered down to examine the imprints in the earth outside the back door. Not surprisingly, there were plenty of horse tracks, boot tracks, wheel tracks, even dog tracks, criss-crossing every which way. Ki had to take his time to sort out the muddle, patiently scanning for patterns that seemed to match the size and weight, as best he could recall, of Quinby and Jessie's horses. Shortly he untangled a set of tracks which had a cracked left foreshoe—the hostler had said the Trigueño had a cracked shoe—and then Ki found where another horse slid its right rear hoof when turning, which Ki recalled was a habit of the mare's.

He was gazing at their trail spearing away through the rear alley when the others arrived from their fruitless searching.

"Nary a sign," Major Thinnes reported. "Miss Starbuck is nowhere in Riverton; I'm dead positive of it."

"I even checked Boot Hill, to see if any new grave had been dug," Mulhollan said, laying a paternal hand on Ki's shoulder.

Adele nodded ruefully. "It shows you the breed of devil we're bucking."

Ki pointed out what he'd discovered, his narrowed eyes holding a desolate look as he replied, "I'm going to track them. I'm going to find Quinby and get Jessie back if I have to search every inch of ground from here to Canada. And if Quinby and his cronies hurt her, God help them. Because I'll kill every last one of them."

Chapter 10

Gradually Jessie's tortured brain groped back to consciousness.

Slanting daylight—she could not be sure whether it was early morning or late afternoon, having lost her sense of direction—limned the pitched canvas roof of a large tent. Attempting to sit up, she made the discovery that she was trussed like a cocoon, her arms behind her back, her legs roped at the knees and ankles. A filthy rag had been stuffed into her mouth to gag her.

The gradual increase of sunlight and warmth indicated it was morning. So she had not been knocked out for a considerable period of time, but long enough to miss her abduction from the hotel room and trip to here—wherever *here* was. Chagrin bit deep, mortification over what Jessie felt to be her lack of vigilance. To be conked witless by a chamber maid was utterly inexcusable.

Woozy, disoriented, she grew more aware of her surroundings. The tent was unfurnished except for a cot in one corner, covered with a buffalo robe, and a table made of hand-hewn lumber on which were piled papers and miscellaneous objects—tobacco tins, whiskey bottles, greasy decks of playing cards. A lantern hung from a roof support pole. She recognized her pistol and shell-belt draped carelessly over a pole brace. A butcher knife jutted from one corner of the table, beside a stale loaf of bread. If she could get to her feet, back up to that blade and saw loose her bonds—

In the act of drawing up her legs, steeling herself for the agonizing effort of standing up, Jessie heard boots approaching across rubble outside. She fell back and closed her eyes, squinting through barely opened lids to watch. The canvas entry flag pulled aside, and Oscar Pascal ducked into the tent, Sheriff Quinby stooping to enter behind him. The men straightened, staring down at Jessie.

"She hasn't come to yet," Quinby said disgustedly.

"No matter," Pascal replied. "She can wait."

"I can't. I hafta get back on the job." Moving to the table, Quinby picked up a canteen and shook it, hearing water slosh. "This bitch an' her sidekick and the major's rooty-tooty stuckup daughter woke me outta sound sleep. They were tryin' to make me tell what I knew of your plans, but I'd of let 'em cut my throat before I'd of double-crossed you, Oscar." He unscrewed the cap and dumped the water over Jessie's face. "Now let's see how well she likes having the same done to her."

Jessie, realizing she could not keep up her pretense of insensibility for an indefinite period, coughed, choked, and finally opened her eyes.

Pascal was facing her, seated close on an upended cartridge case. He jerked the gag out of her mouth. "Woman, you better hope you can answer our questions. That's the one and only reason you didn't die at the hotel in Riverton."

"Things are a li'l different, eh?" Quinby jeered. He'd tossed the canteen aside and now brandished the butcher knife. "It's your tongue that's in for a shaving now, if you don't talk!"

Pascal, his face only a trifle less cruel of mouth and eye than that of the brutal sheriff at his side, grinned as Quinby jabbed the knife at Jessie's eyes, forcing her to writhe frantically in her bonds. "Where'd Ki and Miss Thinnes go? Were you expecting them back? Who with?"

Jessie, in her debilitated condition, could find only the strength to return Pascal's steely glare without flinching.

"Let me carve off her ears," Quinby snarled.

Pascal turned to Quinby and nodded. The sheriff reached for Jessie's right ear and touched the sharp blade to its lobe.

At that instant, the sound of a galloping horse pounding up a rocky slope outside the tent caused Pascal and Quinby to jump to their feet, jerking pistols from holsters, their sadistic plans for Jessie momentarily forgotten. Then they relaxed as through the tent flap plunged Reno, still in his unkempt cavalry uniform.

"I forgot we're safe here, even if Miss Starbuck did discover our hideout." Pascal laughed. "Sit down, Reno. Did you bring some news?"

"Yeah, howdy," Reno grunted, nodding at Pascal and Quinby. "Sergeant Neville's gotten a message that the Box M's duplicate herd is en route to Riverton, and should arrive this afternoon sometime."

Pascal scratched his jaw. "What'd Neville do about it?"

"Not much; he didn't know what exactly to do. He had to pass it on, o' course, but he reported the shipment as due in tonight or even tomorrer so's to stall long enough for me to get instructions."

Pascal thought a long moment before ordering Reno. "Go tell Neville that now is the time for our men to desert and move to our ranch in Montana. Tell him that we'll bid the army g'bye by rustling this second Box M herd like we did before."

Reno licked his lips nervously.

"Well?" Pascal demanded. "What's wrong?"

"I-I could lie and tell yuh nuthin'," Reno answered, staring down at his feet. "Course, I risk my neck ever' time I sneak inside Fort Washakie. But that ain't botherin' me, boss. I can slip through them sentries and palaver with Neville. It's this business of stealin' another Box M shipment that strikes me as dangerous."

Pascal scowled. "Dangerous? We ran into no danger when we grabbed off the first herd. This time it'll be easier and faster. We'll still have to use the ramps and portable chutes to transfer the herd to our train, but we won't have the work of switching scrubs for the prime beef or replacing the seals on the cattle cars."

Reno shrugged, his jaw outthrust sullenly. "What if Major Thinnes tumbles to our deal? He'd send a company o' cavalry pronto to wipe us out."

"Has his daughter or that Chink shown up at the fort?"

"No, not that I know of."

"Well, none of m'boys have reported them two at any river crossing yet," Jessie heard Pascal reply, and relief surged through her at the thought that Ki and Adele had escaped his death traps so far. Then her pulses quickened as Pascal continued. "They're dead meat, Reno; nuthin' can save 'em. M'boys have standin' orders to liquidate 'em on sight. And less'n they blab to the major, he won't wake up to us. Remember, all the while I was in prison, you'n Neville and the others whittled away at the Indian reservation herds, smack under Thinnes's nose without him ever findin' out."

"Yeah, but what if he sends cavalry along anyhow, jus' on gen'ral principles to make sure the train gets to the fort with the beef?"

Pascal waved Reno's fears aside. "It's true I planned only one raid on the Box M. It's true we couldn't get away with substituting scrubs for prime stock more'n once. But things are going well, and the army will never catch you, soon's this is done and you change your name, eh? Don't forget, we're trying to found a ranch of our own. I've already got a crew chousing the first Box M herd on its way north, and if we're ever checked by the law, they'll find only LXD cattle."

"Yuh're the boss, Pascal," Reno answered. "Neville an' the boys'll be glad to leave Fort Washakie. But I still got my doubts about liftin' another shipment from the Box M. Even if we run the mining train back into the tunnel and seal it up again, Major Thinnes's scouts are liable to unearth our hideout—just like *she* an' her pals did."

"Let 'em. They'll learn nothing." Pascal laughed mirthlessly as he rose. "We'll be long gone. Fact is, soon's we raise steam in the ol' locomotive and rig the equipment at the siding for the cattle swap, we're leavin' this hideout for keeps. Coming, Quinby?"

The sheriff's eyes flashed malevolently. "Before you get to countin' your cows, how about my payoff of only one cow—this damn heifer, to be exact?"

Pascal shot a glance at Jessie and said maliciously, "You kill her and we hafta dump her. Why not dump her and let her die slow instead? Pitch her in that poisoned well outside, why not. If she don't drown, the arsenic will fix her."

Jessie, too weak to offer much resistance, moaned as the burly sheriff hauled her to her feet and flung her over a brawny shoulder. Pascal ducked out of the tent, followed by Quinby, who carted Jessie's poundage with no apparent effort.

Orienting herself by the proximity of the holding pens, Jessie saw that the tent was one of the group she had spotted the previous night, just before her initial capture by Pascal. He headed for the tunnel which concealed the cattle train. Reno, mounted on a leggy mustang, trotted after Pascal on his way to Fort Washakie to advise Pascal's army confederates of their plans for later that same day. Quinby carried her along the ledge, away from the tunnel and tents, to a circular stone combing of a well.

"This's better, I reckon, but I wouldn't have minded

carvin' you like a Christmas goose, you slut," Quinby snarled, halting at the rim of the open-top well. "So's you won't feel too lonesome, this here's where Ki will be put in to pickle, 'fore long."

Jessie felt herself plummeting through space, to land with a foamy splash in brackish water ten feet below ground level. Her trussed legs hit bottom, and she was standing in armpit-deep water. The rock wall of the well, most likely dug and later abandoned by the original Zenoble miners, was crusted with a greenish smear, which told Jessie that arsenic deposits were in this water. The poison-infused water would kill her if thirst drove her to take a drink.

Peering up at the white disk of the Wyoming sun, she saw Quinby's head and shoulders above. Then the diabolical sheriff vanished from sight.

Chapter 11

At the west edge of Riverton, Adele and Major Thinnes reined in while Ki dismounted yet again to study the ground.

Imprints of a cracked foreshoe headed westbound on a small horse path. Satisfied that they had been made by Sheriff Quinby's Trigueño, Ki remounted, and the three riders continued at a careful jog for a couple of miles. Just before a wedge of cottonwood, the only trees in the vicinity, the path angled northward, and Ki spotted where the Trigueño and another horse had left the path and continued overland.

For a while their horses trotted over waves of low hills, but about the time they passed into a region of jumbled foothills, the tracks disappeared in the dry, rocky rubble that stretched to another tier of hills in the near distance. So far, Quinby had been aiming more or less due west, his greatest variations being around or through difficult terrain. There was nothing ahead that appeared menacing enough to avoid, or attractive enough to turn for, and by now Ki was nursing a suspicion as to the sheriff's destination. So Ki kept them moving straight, though they often dismounted to search for marks of that telltale shoe or any other indistinct sign of passage.

When they were nearing the hem of the second tier of hills, Adele called attention to a pale drift of smoke she'd glimpsed to the south. It was scarcely more than a gossamer thread curling above the buttes along Wind

River, but it was moving eastward at a rapid clip, and was not difficult to identify.

"The work train from the fort," Thinnes stated, frowning quizzically. "I guess word came that the Box M shipment reached Riverton ahead of schedule, and a detail from Third Platoon are under steam to pick it up."

"Or p'raps my herd pulled in on time, and your platoon knew when to expect it but tol' you different," Mulhollan responded sardonically.

Onward they toiled, Ki persistently scrutinizing the difficult terrain . . . ferreting the occasional hoofprint, the white scratch of iron shoe against stone, the cracked twig still pithy green inside . . . deciphering the trail slowly and painstakingly until, descending through a straggly belt of tamarack, they entered the pocket valley which had contained the dubiously branded LXD cattle.

They had arrived by a more direct route than they'd left the *vallecito;* Sheriff Quinby evidently was no stranger to its location. They found signs of his and Jessie's horses, in part impressions and disturbed grasses; and many more signs of cows having cropped and crapped throughout the valley. But there was not an animal of any sort anywhere to be seen. Following the horse tracks, they loped across the deserted valley to the canyon, where the prints dissipated into the raw-chewed earth of the cow trail.

"Easy now," Ki cautioned, as they wound toward the line camp.

Quietly, rifles were drawn from saddle boots and laid handy across laps while they slowly, warily, proceeded through the canyon. Upon approaching the old slab hut, it looked more ruined, more decrepit, than Ki and Adele remembered, and it was quickly determined to be bare-walled vacant.

Immediately Ki began examining the packed earth around the front. Jessie had been taken to the valley as he'd suspected, and presumably she'd been brought to this shack. Now she was gone, disappeared—most likely dead. Yet Ki refused to admit his fears, to accept the obvious, scrupulously working his way out in fanning sweeps toward the lower end of the canyon.

"I'm startin' to wonder if you an' Ki ain't tetched," Thinnes commented skeptically to his daughter. "We've been out huntin' for hours and ain't flushed nary a gunman or lawman or anything what you promised."

"Not even a cow," Mulhollan groused. "Not a LXD, Box M, or mangy brush stray is to be eyeballed hereabouts, like you claimed."

"Nor is Jessie Starbuck. Have you forgotten her?" Adele retorted waspishly. "Where d'you think Ki got that brand from? The herd was here, but as you yourself said, Hep Mulhollan, this's a cattle cache and Pascal has drove them elsewhere. And I dasn't even dream what Quinby's done with poor Jessie."

"Miss Starbuck's vanishment is the only reason I've stuck with your wild goose chase. But," the major warned Adele, "if it turns out you're actin' like flibbertigibbets—or worse, if you're tryin' to tarrydiddle me—y'all will get charged full blame and I'll punish accordingly."

"Stop squabbling and come here," Ki called, impatience sharpening his voice. He was over by the bend in the canyon where he, Jessie, and Adele had first glimpsed the line cabin, and was squatting to peer at an indented hoofprint. When the others gathered, he showed how the edges hadn't crumbled and still displayed signs of overturned gravel, indicating that the print was as recent as sometime that day. And it had been made by a cracked shoe.

Without lingering, they set off along the cattle trail, tracing it westward through the maze of fields and draws which Ki had once hoped never to visit again. He continued his dogged search, concentrating on off-trail signs, realizing there wasn't much point in studying traces of travel on the beaten course. On occasion he would halt for closer inspection of the shoulders and fringes, but otherwise he kept to his chore as steadily and rapidly as care would permit, squinting hard in the glare of the lowering sun.

Presently they reached the flats where the trail rambled in from the west-northwest. Ki reined in by the dogleg curve there, and, shading his eyes with his hand, stared meditatively at yonder uplands.

Finally Thinnes demanded, "What're you thinking?"

"That I am that name you called me—a dolt, a flibbertigibbet," Ki replied with a peevish sigh. "Obviously Quinby knew more than he confessed to us. He knew where the valley was, knew Pascal cached stock there, and must've figured if he didn't find Pascal there, the line camp crew could tell him where to go."

"I'll more'n tell him where to go," Mulhollan interjected.

"We all will, Hep. Now, the tracks show he and Jessie straightaway took the cow trail, alone. That means Pascal wasn't there—and maybe the crew and herd weren't either— but Quinby knew where to go next to look for him. And I should've known, too—long before now." Ki pointed toward the distant shimmery knolls on the other side of Wind River. "I bet this trail connects to the cattle ford, and Quinby followed it there, crossed, and went up to the mine tunnel."

Adele snapped her fingers. "Sure, that's where Pascal must hang out a lot. His old train is there, after all; and he caught us there, didn't he?"

"The point is, the trail is for herding; it takes a long, easy, scenic route," Ki finished. "We can short-cut to the ford and go over. I may be wrong, and it may lose time and, perhaps, Jessie. But I've a feeling it's an odds-on good chance of being right."

The others agreed. Veering from the trail, they rode toward the hills, Ki and Adele in the fore as they retraced the path they'd forged with Jessie while fleeing the previous night. Ki hoped their sense of direction would not falter, doubting they'd overtake the sheriff and Jessie no matter how well they did, how briskly they pushed themselves. Quinby's lead was too great, and he knew precisely where he was bringing Jessie. Their cavalry mounts and Mulhollan's grulla had been ridden for half a day with scarcely any respite, and now were panting on the grades. More than once, their footing wavered astray. A throbbing weariness weighed upon Ki, and Adele had the appearance of a woman from whom all energy had been drained.

When at last they dropped from the slopes to the river bank, they neared the cattle crossing constantly watchful, cautious to pick terrain that would help conceal them. Reining off into boulders and scrub trees around the ford, each took a turn with Major Thinnes's field glasses to scan the ascending trail, the hillside approaches, and the visible rim of the ledge up across the river.

Shadows were lengthening as sunset grew closer, making it difficult to detect gunmen amid rocks and brush, and what lurked beyond the first few feet of the ledge was anyone's guess. Still, at best they could determine, not a soul was anywhere up along that sloping knoll. The look, the *feel* of emptiness which Ki sensed filled him with bitter dismay, for it boded the odds-on chance of once again having figured wrong.

"We're awful slow, or it's returned awful fast," Thinnes suddenly remarked, while focusing his glasses leftward on a final survey of the area. "And dang me, either I'm twiddled around or these lenses are distorted, 'cause it doesn't seem to be goin' like it should."

Their attention drawn along his line of sight, the others could perceive a puff-beaded string of smoke against the coloring skyline. From the far side of the buttes it rose, and Adele needed to view its streamering ribbon only a moment longer before she corrected her father, rather sharply.

"You're not late, lost, or deluded. That smoke cannot possibly be coming from the work train on its way back to the fort, but from some other engine."

"I always reckoned you saw loco," Mulhollan joshed.

"Very droll," Thinnes snapped. Then he asked, "What other engine?"

Ki said, "The only one it could be, the Zenoble mine train."

"But why—" Thinnes paused, swallowed, then said in a tight voice, "You think they're planning to raid the beef shipment when it passes nearby?"

Before Ki could do more than shrug, anger rose upon Hep Mulhollan and he bellowed, "*What?* Rustle my herd again?" Roweling spurs into his grulla, he launched forward in a wild gallop. "They can't do it! I won't let them!"

"Oh, no!" Ki groaned. Adele cried, "Hep!" and Major Thinnes commanded, "You damn idiot, hie yourself back here before you're shot!"

Unheeding, brandishing his Sharps, Mulhollan splashed recklessly across the ford. Immediately they raced after, plunging furiously as they had the night before through the river currents, chasing him up the serpentine grade to the ledge, bracing expectantly against whipsawing lead. Mulhollan was still ahead, swaying and jerking as his grulla groped for traction, when he crested the trail and tore on, passing momentarily from sight. Still no bullets, no outlaw yells. To their vast relief, they discovered when they topped the ledge that it appeared as entirely abandoned as it had seemed from below.

Mulhollan, they saw, was sheering madly toward the tunnel. They shouted to stop, to no avail. Then his horse lurched, keeling aflank as if both right legs had slid out from under it, catapulting Mulhollan from his saddle while rolling over, legs flailing. Mulhollan sailed tumbling and landed asprawl, motionless, shapeless, on the hard ground.

Frantically they reined in and leaped down. Already the grulla was scrambling upright, thoroughly boogered, and as it wobbled away in a skittish tango of bucks and twitches, they rushed to where Mulhollan lay on his back, arms outstretched, eyes closed. Kneeling, Adele placed an ear to his chest.

"Get . . . off me," Mulhollan gasped.

Adele straightened. "Oh! You're breathing."

"If I is, don't ask more o' me for a while," he wheezed hoarsely, still not moving. "That mis'rable crowbait treacherized me, slippin' an' fallin' on loose gravel, an' now look at it jus' traipsin' off."

"Sounds like its foolish owner," Ki retorted, more than a bit rankled. "You stay put and collect your wits if any, while I scout around."

Walking to where the trail formed at the holding pens, Ki hunkered down and studied the welter of numerous prints back and forth, trying to sort out and piece together the passing action. Tracking, he sometimes thought, was like untangling a skein of yarn, and shortly his practiced eye unraveled the scuffed outline of that cracked foreshoe. Heartened, he sought more. He caught a few, a very few, but they all pointed off-trail toward an area beyond the pens, where some dozen tents were pitched haphazardly among the rocks.

About then Thinnes joined him, toting his saddle carbine and frowning as though miffed. "Listen here, Ki. I've played along 'cause I love m' daughter and have a fond weakness for that cussed ol' warthog, but I'm not blind. Clearly nothing's been found 'cause there's nothing to find. I'm afraid if there'd been, those pesky Inspector-General agents would've sleuthed it out."

"An army investigation is akin to a bison stampede, Major. It chews the ground it covers, I grant, but it runs blindered and unimaginative," Ki said blandly, ignoring the splenetic noises Thinnes made in his throat. "As soon as your I.D. boys figured Hep was guilty, they stopped snooping and aimed at charging him, and quit looking for any other ways to go. They found none, naturally."

"*Izzat so!* Well . . . p'raps it's a mite true, but it doesn't alter the facts. They got 'em, and you don't." Thinnes tugged his spade beard, scowling. "This bein' an open case, I must make a report. I'd hate for my superiors to think a nincompoop wrote it, and I'd hate worser for my service record to note I may be suffering pre-senile dementia. Worstest, Ki, I'd hate not to have the facts to answer them. I want facts, plenty of facts, and facts pronto!"

"Fine. So do I."

The major stiffened as if scalded. "You better have them to give. If you can't, if this's some stunt concocted by you and Miss Starbuck and, Lord help her, my daughter, I'll put all of you to swabbing latrines with toothpicks!"

"The facts are the prints, and the prints go over there," Ki replied affably, motioning toward the clump of tents. He started walking that way alongside the pole fencing of the pens, and Thinnes fell in step, muttering darkly. Ki felt a prod of warning, an intuitive sense of something amiss, which under the circumstances did not surprise or alarm him. Still, he slowed, scanning sharply, and suggested, "Keep your eyes peeled and your carbine jacked."

"Already am, rookie. Great spot for ambush. Still, I suspect we'd have burned fire before now if snipers were hereabouts. What d'you see?"

"Nothing. Not even prints coming back, which likely means nothing, too. It's probably deserted as it looks, and Quinby's taken Jessie on ahead or gone around by-passing us, or I may've missed them." Ki shrugged it off as a loose end, but he continually swept his gaze along the striated cliffs, the ledge around and behind, and the bouldered nest of tents they were nearing.

When they cautiously entered the rocky campsite, they found it more dismal than menacing. On one side were remnants of a rockslide and pile of rotten mine timbers, and on the other spread a grassy patch that was watered by a tiny rill splashing from a fissure. The patch was staked off to form a crude corral, but no horses were in it. By the patch, at about the midpoint of the stony pocket, was a communal cookfire mounded with cold ashes and refuse. The tents were plunked everywhere else there was level space. Most were seven-foot peaked miner's tents; some were the larger wedge type, a few were of the sizable wall style, and all were a weather-worn drab.

Nothing moved, nothing sounded. It was growing more difficult to perceive detail, however, for the sunset dazzled blindingly, searing anything facing west, and casting everything else in a vermilion haze. The shadows subdued rather than concealed the campsite, which gratified Ki on two counts; it allowed him to see, but it blurred the grubby unkemptness that looked as if it had grown, like tree rings, by layers over the years. Yet that didn't explain Ki's latent restiveness welling again, alerting, advising care as he and Major Thinnes separated to search the tents.

The checking moved swiftly, there being little to find. The tents were trashed inside and hastily vacated, as though abandoned in panic under doom of vandals or plague. Ki could have believed either excuse, but he chalked it up to the rustlers' being unmitigated slobs.

In one of the large wall tents, he came upon Jessie's shell belt and holstered pistol hanging from a pole brace. It was hardly a shocking discovery; after all, he'd traced her to the camp, yet her weapon was a nice confirmation of her presence, and it pinpointed the exact tent she'd stayed in. Pulse quickening, he scoured the tent, but ended up with nothing more of hers, or any other clue.

After showing her belt and pistol to Thinnes, Ki moved on to other tents. Some had more litter than others, but that only made for more of the same; the scabrous interiors were a monotony of broken and ripped discards, liquor bottles, poker chips, cards, candle stubs, moldy food and suchlike. It was downright depressing, and Ki was becoming downright discouraged, when he heard the major shouting his name.

Diving from a wedge tent, Ki sprang toward the major, who was standing by a dead campfire, scratching his hair and staring across at the grassy patch. Where the rill flowed out through the makeshift corral, a horse was languidly nuzzling a drink. It was the first and as yet only horse they'd spotted, and that alone would have made the moment interesting for Ki.

What really intrigued Ki, however, was that the horse was a liverish hammerhead mare. It was geared ready to ride, save for the saddle, which was loose-cinched, lacking a carbine in its boot and Jessie in its hull.

"Where'd it come from, Major?"

"Search me. I saw 'er when I came out of m' last tent."

Ki went over and looked the mare over. It stood splay-footed and saggy, its neck drooping and its muzzle sucking noisily at the water. Dust lay like flaxen snow over its body and gear, proof of its having been ridden hard and far. But it was not lathered or blowing, not even breathing hard; indicating it'd had time to recuperate since its rigors. Ki spotted no injuries, no blood from any source, nothing worse than a loop of rope tied to one stirrup and cut off at the knot. Minor though it was, it attested to Jessie's having been bound and kidnapped aboard this mare.

"I eat my words, Ki, if I implied Miss Starbuck was in on a prank," Thinnes said ruefully. "D'you think she may've fled and met an accident?"

"Anything's possible. But if she'd escaped on this mare, the cinches would be tight. You loosen 'em when resting a mount for some while, but the mare wouldn't have drifted on its own. It must've been set loose."

"By Quinby. Miss Starbuck would've hightailed. Wonder why he did?"

Ki didn't reply, dreading his answer. Quinby would have freed the mare when he had no more use for it, meaning when Jessie had no more use for it; and that'd be when Quinby had no more use for Jessie. Maybe not, maybe there was another answer; but this seemed the likeliest. Ki trusted in probabilities to guide life and decide death, although he also believed in miracles the way gamblers believe in lucky streaks. Still, nobody beat the odds over the long haul. But Ki refused to voice his apprehensions, not while any hope or faith remained that Jessie might win her high-risk bet.

Thinnes asked, "Any notion, any guess where she might be?"

Dead, Ki thought grimly, but he responded. "Offhand, Jessie might be where she parted company with her horse. It returned here for water, indicating it wasn't freed at a terribly far distance. From the west, I'd say; since both sides are fierce climbs, and Adele knows the mare and would've called if it came by there." Squinting into the sunglare, Ki began across the campsite, grit and pebbles crunching underfoot. "So as a guess, Major, Jessie is in this general region a short way west of here."

Thinnes nodded glumly as he walked alongside. "I'm afraid when we find her, Ki, Quinby will be long skipped for parts unknown. That's my guess."

"Perhaps you should take everyone back to the fort,"

Ki suggested. "If search patrols could be dispersed quickly enough, they might be able to run Quinby to ground, and they'd sure make looking for Jessie simpler."

"I was thinking the same, Ki. You'll come with us, of course?"

Ki shook his head, moving on. Ahead were only some hardy bushes leaching an existence from the flinty, boulder-strewn soil, enflanked by brooding cliffs. It wasn't much, but it brought him that much closer to Jessie, and that was what he told Major Thinnes, adding determinedly, "Once Jessie is found, once whatever needs doing for her is done, then if Quinby is still at large, I'll go hunting. How long it takes, where it takes me, doesn't matter. I plan to be there to welcome him on the start of his slide to hell—"

An unearthly, echoing cry came to Ki's ears in that moment, a sepulchral sound which seemed to issue, ghostlike, from the very ground on which they were standing.

"Ki! Ki, help me!"

Wheeling, astonishment bedazing their features, Ki and Thinnes headed in the direction of the feeble voice. Loudly, Ki yelled encouragement, and in response, the hollow reverberations helped guide them to their source. Angling toward the cliffs, they swiftly wove between clumped boulders, and navigated a twisty sweep that brought them to a small clearing by the cliff. It was there that Ki and Thinnes located the black maw of the arsenic-tinctured well.

"Get me up out of here!"

The next moment they were gazing down into the murky depths. Twilight mottled the disk of water ten feet below, and they saw Jessie's anguished face peering directly up at them. "Hold on!" Ki shouted to her. "I'll be right back with a saddle rope. I'll crawl down after you. Don't go away!"

The response Jessie gave Ki's last gem of advice was

pitched too low to be heard. Probably just as well; Major Thinnes might have been scandalized by her pithy expletive, which young ladies of good breeding weren't supposed to know, much less utter.

At a dead run Ki and Thinnes returned for their horses. Adele, relieved to see them and joyed to hear of Jessie, promptly joined them. A fully recovered Hep Mulhollan was stumping about trying to catch his fractious grulla. "I'll get it tamed quick," he promised them, fuming. "I'll be a-straddlin' that rackabones and ridin' after yuh in two ticks, you'll see."

Leaving Mulhollan hot on the chase, the three headed back at a gallop, Ki pausing to fetch along the mare by its reins. The mare, like Ki's gelding, had come equipped with ranch cast-offs, including a lasso rope no better than his. This Ki saw clearly at the well, where the Thinneses kept Jessie company while Ki unwound both old ropes, examining them as he did so and wondering why bother. They were worn to the core, the sisal braiding flaky dry and fraying apart. Mulhollan had a stout coil on his grulla, not that it mattered, and the cavalry rigs supplied by Thinnes carried no ropes. It boiled down to two bad ropes being better than nothing, if only marginally. Considering whose necks would be soon risking them, Ki knew damn well why he bothered.

Next, postioning his and Jessie's horses near the well, Ki discussed with Thinnes what to do, as he tied a rope to each saddlehorn. He then went to the well and flipped the rest of both ropes over the edge, and after a swift check and a high sign to Thinnes, he grabbed a rope and swung into the well.

"Catch me if I fall!" he yelled, starting to ease downward.

"Don't you dare!" Jessie called. "I hope you know what you're doing."

"Sure. This is the same as hauling a horse out of

deep water," Ki replied. For the next few feet he heard only silence from below, and the whip of rope through his hands and the thump of his feet against the stone walls as he swung and dropped, swung and dropped, in a rhythmic routine.

Finally Jessie said, "Just for that, I shouldn't warn you about the arsenic. The sides are green with it, and the water here is sheer poison."

"Now she tells me." He continued his descent unchanged, snuggling the rope around his wrists and bracing his feet against the sides, until he reached the water. Slowing, he dipped lower till he could stand, taking great care not to cause any splash or spray.

Jessie waded closer, enervated by her long battle against unconsciousness and drowning in the lethal water. "First off, cut these ropes," she begged.

"Turn around," Ki said, whipping out one of his knives. Swiftly he slashed the cords binding her arms behind her back.

She immediately went to work on reviving her cramped muscles and circulation. "Don't try freeing my legs," she said. "It's far too dangerous, and I can wait till we get up top."

"That one I won't argue," Ki said, eying the bilious water as he pocketed his knife. He then wound one of the ropes around Jessie and knotted it so that it fashioned a sling up under her arms. "I'll take the other rope. You hold tight to me and we'll go up together." *If the ropes don't break,* Ki thought to himself, yanking on his to signal the Thinneses.

The ascent went smoother than Ki could have hoped. The major and his daughter gradually drew them to ground level, each teamed with a horse and guiding it to pull on its rope with a matching slow and steady rate. Ki had his rope serpentined around one arm, his other arm around Jessie's waist. She clung to him, hugging him, woefully aware of the poisonous plunge should anything go wrong. But by midway, much of her old assurance had returned, and by the rim, she was actually beginning to relax and enjoy it for what it was worth, which in a great sense was her own life.

Still, she felt relieved when finally hands tugged her free of the hole and onto the bordering grass. Ki was right behind, and he speedily cut the ropes on her knees and ankles while Adele played nurse and felt Jessie's pulse. Hep Mulhollan, who'd arrived on his grulla during their ascent, hovered close with a dolorous expression, clucking his tongue and shaking his head.

"We'll have to forgo the pleasure of pursuing and capturing Sheriff Quinby," Major Thinnes said. "You may've drunk the waters accidental, or inhaled too many gases and vapors down there, Miss Starbuck. Why, you could even be dyin'; we don't know. I'll have you checked into the fort infirmary the moment we return."

"Nuts," Jessie replied succinctly. "I'm very thirsty, is all."

The major brought his canteen, and while Jessie quenched her parched innards, the others spoke tersely, sketching the events since leaving her with the sheriff. Jessie was sitting up straight by time they finished, but was wincing some as she gingerly felt her left temple. It was a raw goose egg, pulpy from the maid's sneak attack or from one or more of the other clouts she'd received along the way.

"Are you sure you're okay?" Adele asked solicitously.

"I'm sure," Jessie replied, managing a smile. "A twister of a headache. Other than that, nothing in particular feels snapped or broken."

"What luck," Mulhollan said.

Luck. That unpredictable joker in the game, Ki thought as he heard Jessie begin recounting her capture by Quinby. She'd been unfortunate to have been waylaid by Delores, but highly fortunate not to have been murdered, and have them come along in time. Come to consider, it was unlucky for Mulhollan to have taken his hard spill and very lucky that he'd missed serious injury. How do you gauge happenstance? How can you figure coincidence—such as Jessie's good luck in eavesdropping on Pascal, which stemmed from her bad luck in being captured and taken to die. You can't. You can only play such wild cards the way fate deals them.

Ki listened attentively as Jessie related how Pascal had outlined his plans, including the impending raid on Box M's replacement herd. "No time to go into detail," he heard her exclaim impatiently. "It's such a simple job to change the U.S. iron into the LXD that Pascal decided our duplicate shipment is a prize ripe for the plucking. He's having Neville withdraw their men from the fort tonight, and plans to chouse cows and crew up to his Montana spread, where he can market his rustled, blotch-branded beef without fear of detection."

"Skunk-blooded pack o' sidewinders," Major Thinnes declared. "I got my facts straight, Ki; I got my answers okay."

Jessie, leaning on Ki's arm, rose to her feet while saying to the major, "We'll get lots more, if we can get to that railway siding in time."

"There's only one small section where the tracks divide and run parallel," Thinnes replied. "But Miss Starbuck, I'm afraid we'll be too late."

"I'd hate to not try and find out we wouldn't have been too late."

"I'm hearing flint in your voice again," Ki told her, and gave a small sigh. "We've got to leave here, true enough, before the whole mob comes pouring out the tunnel. But going out after them? Jessie, think again."

"Don't tell me to think again. Not when I've spent a day in poison with nothing else to do but think. Not when the man who ordered me thrown in the well has swiped one herd from me and's swiping another while I stand here arguing." Jessie's arm was not as steady as usual, but she buckled on her shell belt with impulsive determination. "And not when the outlaw lawman who did the tossing, among other things, is probably right in there with them."

"Quinby," Ki said, his eyes flaring.

"Mighty persuasive," Thinnes murmured. "We could reconnoiter . . ."

"We could do lots of things," Jessie said, twitching her pistol in her holster, regarding the major adamantly, with the proud, unflinching stubbornness that had been a Starbuck trait for generations. "Perhaps we could do what we should do, and that's to stop them dead in their train tracks."

Chapter 12

Soon, with Major Thinnes directing the way, they swept eastward across the ledge and passed beyond the tunnel. From the low foothill cluster comprising the graveyard, they climbed a twisty maze of animal paths and overland jogs while the last rays of the sunset dappled the terrain with cinereous light.

Eventually they topped the ridgeline. The descent along the southern flank of the buttes was not too steep, yet in total their route was taking an arduous toll of time and energy. However, the alternative was to use the mine tunnel and follow the tracks awhile, an easier course which could suddenly, without warning, prove extremely costly. Alert, they moved on, the major riding point. After short stretches of several faint trails, they glimpsed Lance Puheska's place. No lights could be seen, nor sheep or sheep dogs, the only visible movement being the tin vanes of his windmill slashing at the gathering dusk. For some while longer they continued traversing ridges and dipping through ravines, until finally they emerged into a sloped, scrubby ravine which resembled most all the ravines that had come before it. Major Thinnes, however, found it distinctive enough to call a halt.

His voice was low. "The siding isn't far, now. Keep quiet."

Dismounting, they took up their reins and tugged their horses forward and downward. The minutes seemed to crawl, fraught as they were with potential danger while they descended through growth and rubble to where they could see without being seen, able to hear, as they neared, the faint noises of men. They worked lower, toward the tracks, with horses muzzled, weapons cocked, ears tuned for sounds of approach, and eyes searching the rocks choked with spindly timber and thorny growth.

At last, by cautiously parting a brush hedge, they caught view of the railway running through a cleft in the lower slopes. The passage was broad, shallow, eroded like a centuries-dry riverbed, forming a natural course for the parallel tracks of the main line and the siding.

Ahalt there sat the army engine and fort-bound cattle train. Across on the siding, the string of makeshift stock cars was parked with the old mine locomotive facing town. Steam panted from the boilers, smoke chuffed idly out the stacks. The headlamps and side markers were not lighted—and no wonder. Pascal, Sheriff Quinby, a dozen-odd henchmen, and as many or more outlaws in blue uniforms were in the strip between trains, busily and efficiently rustling the Box M herd.

"Why, I'll have those traitors before a firing squad before—" Major Thinnes broke off, sputtering, his face purpling. He fisted his powerful hands and said, "First we'll have to go back to the fort. Two mounted companies should be plenty, but I'll field a battalion if need be."

"By then they'd be halfway to Montana," Jessie countered. "You can see they've almost finished their roundup here. We don't have the time."

As if to underscore her statement, three rustlers hastened to the last cattle car. Using a prybar, they broke the aluminum strip which the Natrona yard master had used in sealing the locked handle of the sliding doors. Other men hurried over with plankboards and bolts of canvas. In moments they had the car opened, a ramp erected, and a crude sort of cattle chute rigged across to an empty stock car of the mining train.

"I'd never've dreamt o' funnelin' cows," Mulhollan commented, hunkering near Ki. "But it reasons to be faster 'n' quieter than chousin' 'em, 'specially without horses to help. O' course, scheming up cow-thefts using that ol' diamond-stack steamer they found, now *that* is getting too damn clever,"

Ki nodded. "Unusual, too, for outlaws to plan and wait so long. I hadn't thought of Pascal as a shrewd boss, but while he was in jail, his men worked to build him the rustling ring he now leads. Those who didn't enlist made their camp at the mine, and one of them, Moulton, claimed they cleared the tunnel over a year ago, which probably was when they fixed the locomotive. They ran it—it was heard— but not on a big haul until Pascal got out and got set. I think you just chanced to be the first along after they were all prepared, ready to substitute those ganted culls. Those were no doubt rustled too, a few at a time, wherever they could be found."

"They couldn't be rustled. Nobody would admit to owning 'em," Mulhollan groused, eyeing his prime stock file blundering along the flimsy chute. "I reckon the switch was like this but in reverse. The scrubs were drove from the cow cache to the mine, trained to here, and p'raps another chute was hitched up so cars on both trains could empty 'n' fill, back 'n' forth, in sequence."

"Makes sense. Doors were relocked, the seals easily forged—and since Neville's job was to break them, I bet he dumped the fakes, and turned in the genuine seals he'd saved from here. Meanwhile, your herd was shunted to the mine and hoofed down to the cache for alterations—"

The slam of couplers and drawbars interrupted Ki. A rattling shudder passed down the cattle train, and two tardy rustlers leaped from the last car, taking the ramp with them. This end of the chute tilted, half-collapsed on one side, but across at the exit end, the chute was a-jostle with bawling cows yet to be loaded. The empty cattle train, pushed by a gustily puffing army engine, began to roll backwards slowly. This surprised the five watchers above, for they expected the rustlers simply to abandon the looted train. It took them a second to catch on. The front of the train blocked the down-track switch of the siding, and had to be backed past the switchpoint to let the loco's haul of beef-bulging stock cars leave for the mine.

Ki's first thought was optimistic: *Till the switch opens, the beef stays. Well, that's obvious,* he thought next . . . yet it prompted him to consider that point down there as one that might well be worth taking . . .

Jessie's first thought was pessimistic: *When the switch opens, the beef goes. It's a deadline, no ifs, no maybes, and almost no time.* That immutable fact was gall to swallow, and her tanned face was bleak, her eyes arctic green. "It's up to us. We've got to stop them."

"Jessie, m' heart howls like a wolf," Mulhollan growled. "But m' eyes see all them bluebelly rustlers down there who're desertin' their army careers forever, t'night, to join them other hombres in troublesome pursuits. That's three excuses for 'em to kill; another is our beef, and they don't need it none. M' head says whoa up, but m' ears wanna hear how you'll stop them from drivin' our stolen herd wherever they choose to drive it."

"We've got to do more than just stay roosted here!"

Major Thinnes gave an exasperated sigh. "I thought my wife was blue-mule stubborn, and my daughter is a balker, too. But without a doubt, Miss Starbuck, you are the most obstinate, hard-headed female ever born!"

"In other words, I'm to accept meekly the short end of the deal a second time?" It was a rhetorical question; she answered it herself, looking glum. "In other words, yes."

"In other words," Ki said, rubbing an ear, "maybe no. We're sunk here, but we may have one last crack at the Zenoble mine branch. If we beat the train there, then open the main-line switch while the cars are crossing the frogs, we should derail at least one car."

Adele spoke up. "I like the idea, and think it's worth a try. But Ki, what'll we do when the rustlers swarm down to investigate the derailment?"

"Keep riding," her father responded. "We'd best've left by then, like when the initial confusion breaks. Otherwise we'll never make it to our horses."

Jessie nodded her approval. "It won't get very many of them, but it will stop them from stealing another Box M herd. And I'll accept that."

They began their withdrawal from the brushy hedge, seeing that the rustlers were about to make theirs. All but the nose of the creeping cattle train was up-track of the siding switch. The Rustlers' Express was loaded to overcapacity with Box M's choicest steers, and the car doors were being shut a final time.

Every moment was crucial. Deciding to approach the Zenoble branch-line switch by riding the trackline, rather than by following a safer but more roundabout course through the hills, they quietly eased their horses along a slope until they were beyond danger of the rustlers.

They were still well above the tracks, although they could glimpse the twisting bends of steel now and then, and at the first opportunity presented by the terrain, they bore descending to the right-of-way. They blazed their own trail, weaving through the indistinct scrub and rock, clawing along steep banks and declivities where their horses almost slid on their hindquarters.

Shortly, threading their way through a tangle of brush and trees, they reached the shoulder of the tracks. They eased over a ditch onto the cinder bed of the railway, whose twin steel lines snaked more or less westward.

After a swift glance about, they rode the trackline at a steady gallop, often peering back over their shoulders, their ears attuned to the approach of a steam engine. Dusk fell softly, quietly, as they continued riding through the seemingly endless succession of gulches and canyons.

At last they came to where some of the rougher country spilled down across the basin. Major Thinnes turned suddenly from the trackline and led the way down a wash that was dry as a bone. He cut from that into a larger gulch full of boulders, and soon from there he climbed through a steep draw and reined in.

"The rustlers probably didn't post a guard at the switch, but I wasn't in a mood to find out too late," Thinnes said. "We're back in behind it, and if you recall how that area looked, it's awful open for mounted riders. C'mon, we can move our horses closer, but we'll have to walk them."

Agreeing, the others swung out of their saddles. Single file, they led their mounds as they continued breaking path. Soon they came upon a large depression where, centuries before, a boulder had dislodged and crashed down, leaving a sheer and natural pocket. Anchoring their horses' reins with rocks, they removed carbines from saddle boots and spare ammo from saddle bags, packed the weaponry as best they could, and crawled up to the rim.

Ki said, "I hear the train."

Cupping her ears, Jessie too caught the sound of a locomotive's exhaust as it spun its drive wheels over the tracks. There was no sign of it yet—indeed, unless the engine managed a miraculous end-for-end swap, they should see the tag-end of stock cars first, and the old diamond-stack last.

They started down the other side, toward the switchpoint. It was dark now, and the pale quarter-moon and powder of stars cast meager light. Darkness blurred the rugged harshness of the terrain; the depression in which the branching tracks lay was swathed in gloom, falling away from the tiered ridges in black, corrugated smudges of boulders and thickets. Across the depression they moved like ferrets, testing each step for noise, as they worked their way toward the bushy fringes and drainage ditches around the track beds.

They reached a tangle of scrub junipers still off from the switch, but even now the iron rails were humming to the approach of the mine locomotive.

Ki started forward, paused, and turned to the others. "I can make it quicker alone," he said, handing Jessie his carbine for safekeeping. "There isn't time for all of us to make it, and no need."

Major Thinnes held out a hand to restrain Hep Mulhollan, who was moving into the open. "Let Ki handle the switch, Hep," he cautioned. "We can do more good by siding him while he's in the open."

Unencumbered by the saddle carbine or a pair of heavy boots, Ki skimmed across the ground, gauging his best approach. As soon as he reached the railside ditches, he glided along the edge of the brush until he was within a dozen feet of the Zenoble mine branch. He burrowed into the sheltering brush that thicketed there by the right-of-way, expectant but not tensed, wondering peripherally whether the rustlers had bothered to close the switch or leave it open when they'd steamed down through here earlier that evening. From his standpoint it made little difference, assuming a switchman hadn't stuck around.

He did not have long to wait. Squinting through the moonlight, he saw the rear of the train ease around the bend from the east. There were no lights, and he could hear the locomotive wheezing and clanging way up at the hidden front of the train. The train grated to a halt. A burly outlaw ran from the train toward the switch, clutching a lighted railway signal lantern. He leaped over to the switch lever, cranked the red disk around to right angles to the main line to open the branch track to the Zenoble mine. Then he sprinted over beside the train where presumably the engineer could spot the signal, and waved the lantern in wide arcs, indicating the switch was open.

The cars crunched and squealed, beginning to move again. The burly rustler hurried back to the switch as the rear cars were rattling over the switch frogs onto the branch line. He swung the lantern like an incense burner, shouting good-natured lewdities at the blue-clad rustlers who rode the roofs of the stock cars. They had climbed up there for a serious purpose, ready to set the hand brakes to check the train's momentum or that of a runaway car, but their obscene yells rang through the night as they hurrahed the switchman in return. Ki was starting to wonder if he'd have to remove that outlaw clown when a sidekick reached out and the switchman leaped aboard the passing car.

The mine locomotive had shunted nearly half of the crowded makeshift stock cars onto the branch track now. This would be about as good as he'd get, Ki figured. Paying little heed to the peril of being spotted by the car-riding men, he crawled out into the open alongside the railroad track and scuttled over to the switch.

Gripping the iron lever of the switch, he threw his strength against the jutting iron, timing the movement when the switch frogs were clear of moving wheels. After closing the rusty switch, he dived back into the brush. There was an ear-shattering squeal of iron wheels against steel rails. Wood strained and buckled as the rear trucks of one stock car remained up the side track while the front wheels swung onto the Fort Washakie tracks.

There was only one possible outcome. Flanged wheels strained against their swiveling pins proved unequal to the surging power of the locomotive, and jumped the tracks. For a dozen feet the derailed wheels crunched over the wooden ties. The engineer, apparently unaware of any difficulty, opened his throttle another notch, spinning his drivers against the unexpected resistance further ahead along the string of cars.

Then, with a grating shriek of rending metal, the derailed car tore free of its coupling and slewed crosswise to the others, blocking both the main line and the mine branch. The Rustlers' Express was hopelessly stalled.

Hoarse shouts of dismay went up from the assembled outlaws. The engineer finally caught on, Ki discerned as he watched the play of action; realizing too late that a derailment had occurred, the engineer closed his throttle and braked to a halt, but not before a second car had jumped the track.

Ki burrowed back through the brush, grinning triumphantly as he rejoined the others. "That ought to keep Pascal from rustling *that* herd," he said with a chuckle. "They couldn't get that track cleared in a week!"

Major Thinnes, with a worried glance at his daughter, started pawing his way back toward the hillside brush. "We've got to get out of here," he called. "All thunderation is going to break loose when they figure out what caused their train to go off the tracks!"

Sprinting across the flat, they plunged up the steep hillside nearest the tracks. Pausing, they looked back. Pascal's rustlers were scrambling around the derailed cars, resembling ants in a plowed-up anthill as they swarmed around the switch. Pascal's frenzied bellow reached across the flat, adding impetus to their desperate climb. "This ain't no accident! Somebody opened the switch while the cars were moving onto the branch!"

Sheriff Quinby, racing up to the switch from the far front of the train, lifted his bull voice in a roar which echoed off the surrounding slopes. "Spread out, fellers! We've gotta find 'em and fast, and no quarter given!"

Hep Mulhollan, less agile than the others scaling the

steep slope ahead of him, chose that moment to cling to an outcropping rock for support. The rock cracked loose and bounded down the slope, narrowly missing a batch of Neville's troopers who happened to have fanned out in this direction.

"There they are!" Quinby shouted, gesturing with his revolver. "After the dirty sons, men!"

Gunshots blasted the night. Ki snarled an angry expletive. They'd lost the advantage of surprise. Bracing themselves against the steep slope, the five levered cartridges into the breeches of their carbines and opened fire on the advancing rustler crew. Suddenly Mulhollan stiffened and collapsed against the slope, doubling in agony.

"Hep!" Jessie cried.

Mulhollan nodded, straightened, and let fly with the Sharps. Its report was deafening, and the face of his target disappeared, the body lurching like a beheaded chicken. "One down," he croaked, chambering a fresh shell. "I'd have hit his heart, only he was wearing his shirt pocket too high."

"Doesn't matter where you hit with that cannon," Thinnes retorted, as he fired his carbine.

Another rustler slumped to the ground. Those nearby the fallen man vanished like a covey of quails in the brush, but not to hunker in hiding. Instead of checking the outlaw attack, the return fire only caused Pascal's gunhawks to fan out and around while bringing their guns to bear on the slope.

Blistering salvoes targeted the five. Lead clipped the brush on all sides, kicking up whorls of grit to sting their faces. Doggedly they struggled toward the rim, alternatively shooting and climbing, their escape slowed but not stalled as finally they gained the rounded crest. Hunching low to avoid being silhouetted, they headed over and down for their horses—

—And stopped, abruptly.

"Lord!" Adele gasped. "Look at them all!"

"With more on the way," Ki added, glancing aside.

Jessie swallowed thickly. "We're cut off."

Chapter 13

Plunged crouching, they saw that Pascal had outmaneuvered them. Rustlers had already come upon the horses, their discovery attracting others to follow, creating a zigzag line stretching to the shoulder of the ridge, as moonlight winked off drawn gun steel.

"Cut off," Jessie repeated in dismay. "And completely surrounded, once they get up the hill behind us."

Major Thinnes nodded. "The best we can do is to take fort in these rocks and stand 'em off until help shows up."

"What help?" Mulhollan grunted, hand pressed to his side.

"Why, Colonel Benteen's troop patrol is bound to come by, and surely Lieutenant Pomfrit will dispatch a search detail."

Mulhollan looked unimpressed. "Let's not hole up lest we hafta."

He moved as he spoke, starting back to the top. The sound of gunfire was growing in length and volume as Pascal's outlaws obeyed orders to spread out and advance up the bank, moving swiftly in a thin, unbroken line, shooting at every shadow to flush their quarry. After Mulhollan sprang up, so did the others, and together they wended quietly along the rimline, their only remaining path of flight.

With a sudden shudder, Mulhollan wilted against a boulder.

Ki, slinging the strapped carbine to his back, leaped

to catch the wounded old rancher. Mulhollan waved go away, but Ki ducked up under the motioning arm and shouldered him, adding a supportive hold around his waist.

Without word or pause, they shoved onward. Ahead, the ridge melded with wilder hills in a steepening push west and north, but before that, there was a bare stretch where a landslide had sheared a long scar from the bank. They were almost across when shots burst out in a sharp rataplan, the searching rustlers having finally spotted them out in the open.

Jessie, Adele, and Major Thinnes returned fire while backing. Their staggered volleys dampened the rush of men up the ridge, the pursuing outlaw gunfire winking against the background of the stalled cattle train. Mulhollan groaned as bullets rained around them; he fought his unsteady gait while Ki gouged his feet for purchase in the choppy, loose-gravel soil. When a seeming eternity later they reached the far side, the three covering them dove right behind into shelter. Keeping low and out of easy range, they stealthily worked deeper along the main seam of hills.

Behind, Pascal and Quinby were leading a rush of men up the ridge. Jessie and Thinnes dallied to greet them in a lead howdy-do. Stymied by the ambush, they scattered howling their baffled fury, but at Pascal's wrathful direction, they circled around and shot at each other till they realized the snipers had vamoosed.

Adele and Jessie disrupted them with the next surprise barrage before scrambling to yet another position, where Adele was sided by her father. The night lengthened, yet still they were forced to fight and run, managing to hold off the stubborn assaults with a series of skillful ploys and counter-attacks. And though they were gradually wearing down the odds, they kept being thrust farther northwestward, never quite able to shake free and head for safety.

Ki was still determinedly supporting, and was somewhat bent under, the weight of Hep Mulhollan. Mulhollan, faring worse, was nearing the end of his endurance when they breached yet another rise and had a view of the terrain beyond. Directly ahead of them was Lance Puheska's sheep ranch, appearing as unoccupied as when they'd glimpsed it earlier that evening.

"If we could make that stone cabin," Major Thinnes panted, "we could stave off a siege!"

"G'wan, no holin' up," Mulhollan choked. "Not on my sake. Get away while yuh can, an' I'll keep 'em backed off. I'm still good for sump'in."

Now it was Thinnes who looked unimpressed. "You must've got plugged 'tween the ears, you lummox." He reached to give Ki a hand.

Carrying the wounded rancher between them, with Adele and Jessie guarding their flanks, they fought their way out of the brush and boulders into a broad, flat pasture which spread to the ranchyard. Five figures striving to hurry over a sheep-cropped field could scarcely go unseen; and indeed they were not missed, as from behind them rose a clamor of shouts and crashes.

This was not the place or the time for stealth. The chase now consisted of thwarted rustlers thirsting to overtake their victims, who in turn were hurrying frantically to reach the cover of the cabin and make what stand they could. Rifle and pistol fire reverberated across the pasture. A slug flicked Jessie's collar and she flinched instinctively. A carbine kicked, and a gunman fell heavily into the brush, blood oozing from a neat hole drilled between his lungs. Another man stood on a boulder, taking careful aim until he toppled backward, having either accidently slipped or been shot by Jessie, she was unsure which . . .

They hit the front stoop, set to bust in the door if locked. It opened so easily that they were swept lurching inside, but it had a crossbar which they promptly slid through the slots. For a few minutes—five, at the outside—they were safe from outlaw gunfire.

Mulhollan was conscious as ever, but in obvious pain. His blood-soaked shirt was removed after a tussle—mainly him balking at bare-chesting afore ladies—but a preliminary examination by the ladies brought a grin to his lips. The bullet, fired from long range, must have been fairly spent when it drilled his right chest. The ribs it shattered had deflected it around his vitals and out clean. To staunch the double wound, two wadded compresses and a bandage of torn strips were fashioned from a clean shirt, which Ki donated on behalf of Lance Puheska. It was the only clean cloth Ki could find; the one-room cabin was spartanly furnished, with Indian blankets for curtains and bedcover, and a few untanned sheep hides that reeked to high heaven.

"Bring on them rustlin' polecats!" Mulhollan bellowed, wrapped tight and rallying. "I'll live to see 'em dead yet, I reckon."

"Hep, you'll outlive us all," Major Thinnes retorted happily. "The devil couldn't take you, and he'd spit you back."

"You're drawin' m' first bead! Whar's my long gun?" Mulhollan staggered up and grabbed his Sharps, which was propped nearby, but his aim wasn't to pot Thinnes. He'd gone for his gun when Ki, his carbine angled out the peep-slot in the door, opened fire on skulking figures caught exposed on the field.

"They're coming in more on the right," Ki advised, levering for another shot. The cabin had only side windows, so Mulhollan lunged for the right one, clearing it with a swipe of his rifle. Adele thumbed bullets into her magazine while crossing to join him. Mulhollan, Adele and Ki, with Jessie and Thinnes at the left window, blasted at the scuttling black forms and saffron flares in the darkness, making their shots count, counting their shots that remained.

Through the racket, they were able to hear Quinby and Pascal, and Neville on occasion, hurling curses and goading the gun crew. Lead poured through the windows, richocheting about and chewing into the walls, as rustlers swarmed along the sides and around the solid rear wall of the back, completely encircling the cabin.

Firing only when they had a sure target, conserving their fast-dwindling supply of ammunition, the five trapped inside forced the closing ring of outlaws to hold cover. A gunman scurrying by Adele's window abruptly let out a cry and clawed a hit shoulder, spurting blood on his calfskin vest. He and another man who had been beside him vanished, swearing, into the night. Mulhollan rammed his Sharps out then, and as its thunderous discharge receded, wails and thrashings could be heard from the area where the men had fled. Ki kept the front-charging gunmen respectful with rapidly levered fire from his porthole. On the left, Jessie drilled a blue uniform through the breast button, while the major demolished the jaw of another treacherous trooper. A third, twisting in from one side, had his cavalry hat punctured in three places, and slapped a hand to his head in a caricature of a salute before keeling over.

More were behind. The odds were dropping one by one, yet the starting odds had been so formidable that it was useless to speculate on stemming the advancing tide. Pascal and Quinby were gathering the men for an all-out charge that would swamp the cabin by sheer force of numbers. When the attack struck, the defenders knew the best they could do would be to take as many rustlers down with them as possible.

Jessie started loading her carbine, only to stop. "I haven't any more than a dozen shells left, Major. How about you?"

"About the same. We'll have to let them get right up close."

"*Let* 'em?" Mulhollan scoffed from across the room.

"How'd you come by that strategy, from Gen'ral Custer?" Adjusting his pistol holster, he leveled his Sharps again and added seriously, "Let 'em. I only wish y'all were gone. I'd get to notch my gunsights on Oscar Pascal before the fall."

Even as Mulhollan spoke, the gun horde was sweeping forward. "Storm that craphouse!" Pascal was yelling. "Stomp them assholes flat!"

Concentrated lead zeroed in on the door and windows as the outlaws tore across the feebly moonlit clearing, then darted in for the front of the cabin. Those closest were trying to shoot and run at the same time, the men behind them not being overly generous with covering fire. Ki fanned a bunch out front, but his swing couldn't aim flat along the wall, toward other men he glimpsed rushing from deep aflank. They were open to the windows, though, where long guns tracked and raked across the sides, although their shooting angles couldn't bear in on the gunhands upfront. Once against that wall, they could press to the door, knowing that the only way they could be fired on would be if someone leaned out—and that would be suicidal.

It was all suicidal. The four at the windows leaned out to try widening their fire range, feeling they had little to lose but finding it didn't much help. Pascal's gang scented victory. The cabin was a hornet's nest of buzzing slugs, noxious with choking, smarting fumes, a fog of powder smoke thickening down from the ceiling; while just outside, the earth seemed to tremble under the pounding boots of killers eager to get in.

They were thumping the front stoop when struck down by gunfire.

Ki, peering out the door slot for a likely target, saw the flashes lance from back at a bordering copse, but assumed they were just more outlaw shots. That impression changed in a split second, as the ragged volley caught the outlaws by surprise. Men dropped as if poleaxed, squalling in pain. All were thrown into confusion, consternation etching their startled faces. If the enfilade did not create even greater havoc, it was because many were still shocked witless, not fully comprehending, when the Indians arrived.

Ki felt his nerves tauten as the bronzed warriors swarmed into view. Tall, sinewy, hawk-nosed, they wore a variety of styles—white man's work clothes, embroidered breechclouts, rawhide thongs and loincloths—depending probably on what they had and liked. They all carried rifles, mostly vintage squirrel poppers. Some had bows and quivers, and a few carried brightly colored shields and lances. They were surging toward the cabin, yipping raucously, riding bareback with bitless rope bridles, their spotted ponies painted with the same war paint which the braves had daubed on their faces.

"What's going on?" Jessie demanded as they clustered around Ki.

Smiling, Ki let them look. "A Shoshone raiding party."

At a cry from Pascal, his men fell back. Jessie got a glimpse of Sheriff Quinby darting alert glances about, but he vanished in the melee before she could aim her carbine out the slot. The rustlers began firing defiantly, hitting a couple of the lead braves, but now bullets and arrows were whipping from the Indians, shredding the grass, along with a few more gunmen.

"They can't do that!" Thinnes snapped. "Against regulations!"

Mulhollan guffawed. "The Injuns rescuin' the cavalry, what a pip!"

Then, whatever else Mulhollan might have joked was lost in gun thunder as they covered the windows again and the Indians closed on the rustlers. There came throaty blasts of the Indians' Spencer carbines, punctuated by the volcanic roar of the Sharps; the staccato reports of the outlaws' weapons, generally Winchesters and revolvers; the sharper crack of the lighter caliber rifles the Indians were firing; the nasty humming swish of their many arrows, the drumming hoofs and hair-raising cries. . . . It was a deafening, roiling storm, all but ignored as targets were tracked and death was meted out.

And it was a hard, quick battle. The howling braves circled about and melded into a single swirling mob, led by a robust figure whom Ki recognized as Lance Puheska. Pascal and his gang were fighting desperately, unable to hold them at bay. It was ironic, Ki mused; Pascal had trapped himself by trapping them. He continued to blaze away from the door slot while precious bullets were triggered carefully from the window. He paused as the gunmen started to withdraw. At the front and sides, they were drawing away, firing spasmodically.

Unbarring the door and flinging it open, Ki loaded his last cartridges and yelled, "Cover me!"

But Major Thinnes was already diving outside, his face showing a strange mix of outrage and wild, feverish exultation. Ki vaulted after, but once past the stoop, he slowed and grinned. Sergeant Neville was no longer behind his blue-coat crew, exhorting them into finishing the stamp-out. His loyal troopers were evaporating around him, scattering wildly for the rocks and brush, and even his chief general, Oscar Pascal, Ki saw, had the sense to run scrambling after them. Neville was left a widening spot all his own.

"Sergeant, you're arrested," Thinnes called. "Surrender."

Neville, his revolver in hand, turned and saw the major. With a startled beat, he raised the pistol and fired at the same moment Thinnes triggered his own service revolver. Ki saw Thinnes flick something like dust or a thread off his uniform, then ear cock his gunhammer for another shot.

The first had been enough. Neville was snatched

from his feet by lead smashing into his pelvic bone, the slug ricocheting up through his intestines and stomach. He landed on his rump, his head wobbling as if shaking to deny that he was dead.

Thinnes stalked on in search of more deserters. Mulhollan clomped out, his face pale and strained, but full of enough gumption to resist restraint. And behind him stepped Adele, looking determined to drag her father back inside before he became a target himself. Relieved to see they didn't need him, Ki scanned for a horse, any horse, as long as it was near, healthy, and his, before Jessie came out. He glimpsed Lance Puheska, waved, and sprinted toward him.

"Wait, Ki, wait!" Jessie cried, appearing at the threshold.

"Can't!" Ki yelled back as he sped for Puheska. "I saw Pascal making a break toward the mine! If he gets through the tunnel, he'll give us the slip!" Then motioning broadly, he tried to signal Puheska that he needed Puheska's mount, which didn't look the quality of his dead black, but more like a scrubby mustanger, nervous and cross-grained, and likely as not a loaner to Puheska.

A gunshot sizzled past him, followed by a yell. He quit gesturing, quick, but didn't slow or turn to check it. The next shot caught his attention, as a revolver reared up and exploded almost in his face. Ki made out the dark outline of a man and sprang, kicking the man in the chops with the heel of his foot, sending him bowling unconscious in the grass. Without breaking stride, Ki pivoted back on course and bounded to Puheska.

"Listen, I need—"

"I know," Puheska said, dismounting. "But this is a hotspur—"

"I know." Sweeping up the rope rein and vaulting on bareback, Ki jabbed the mustanger into moving. He moved. His neck near whipsnapped as the splenetic mustanger launched galloping, and he let it race off its wild-eyed temper as he guided it after Pascal.

He had speed, even if slightly unmanageable. Pascal had a head start, though, and could dodge him if he wasn't watchful. Twice Ki glimpsed him slewing around bulges far to the front, and the first time Ki didn't believe it, but the second glance confirmed it. Pascal also had a horse. Probably swiped from one of the braves, Ki judged. He looked to have a bit of trouble staying aboard, but his mount was stretched-out flying as it scrambled toward the mine. Grimly Ki set himself to run Pascal down, if not before the tunnel then after. Wherever...

Mere moments before, when Ki had darted from the cabin, Jessie stared after him, feeling annoyed yet anxious. Like any true blood brother, he wanted to protect his sister, and like any sister, she resented it.... Even while she worried about his safety, her senses were strung out to hair-trigger alertness. It was then she heard a sudden angry bellow. She recognized the voice as Sheriff Quinby's—a voice maddened with rage and frustration.

"Attack!" Quinby was shouting from the rocks beyond. "We still outnumber them, you pissants! Mow 'em down!"

The remnants of Pascal's rustling ring responded sluggishly. Those alive on the field broke toward the fringing boulders and copses, while those already there floundered higher among the ridges and seams. From their vantages, they blasted down at the converging Indians. They fought like the vicious, cornered rats they were, against Indian prowess as guerrilla fighters. Despite the cover, despite their own superiority in firepower, they were dislodged time after time, forced to retreat farther into the hills. Jessie ran up into the rocks toward the place where she'd heard Quinby yelling, but the sheriff was no longer there. Craning eyes and ears, she searched the crevices and thickets along the slope.

Nothing.

Jessie was about to turn back when the noise of a small gravel slide brought her pivoting to her left. It was just some small bits of shale trickling down a steep bank, yet gazing up to its source, she discerned the silhouette of Quinby scrambling for the rim of the slope.

She called out, "Don't even dream of escape!"

Quinby's response was a revolver shot that went wide.

Jessie ducked anyway, swearing. Quinby had a short yet crucial head start, up a hill that would leave her perilously exposed. But she, like Ki, felt compelled to try stopping such vermin before they could scuttle free, and started climbing after him. The footing in the loose shale was negligible. She could see Quinby above her, hiking steadily, and chanced a pistol shot. It hit close enough for him to react, jerking, then turn and fire at her again.

Jessie dropped flat, hugging the incline. Lifting her head, she saw him moving again, so she rose and thrust upward. The sharp rock slashed at her denims and bit into the flesh of her hands. Quinby fired a third time, but in a desperate attempt to catch up, Jessie plunged in a skittering run diagonally across to a more solid outcrop of stone. Her risk paid off; Quinby had anticipated she'd go to ground again, and responded a heartbeat too slowly when she made her dash instead. His bullet didn't come near.

She began to climb in earnest now. Clawing for boulders and drawing up between them, she pushed higher to grasp yet another, the broken shale still sliding out from beneath her feet if she put too much weight on them. Quinby paused to squat and reload. Jessie used his delay to wriggle up another ten feet. Quinby aimed by the noise of the gravel slipping down from her grappling climb. His bullet clipped the rock next to her left hand, slitting tiny slivers of stone into her flesh. Ignoring it, she groped for the next highest rock, then the next, until, gasping, she reached the crest.

For just a moment she bent, hands on her knees, regaining her breath. Then she darted along the rimline toward the area where Quinby was likely to appear. She slewed around a small bramble thicket, almost losing her balance again as her boots coasted on the pebbly ground. Quinby was stumbling over the edge, one hand clutching for support—any support—while the other held his revolver. They saw each other almost simultaneously.

"You!" Quinby snarled. "If it hadn't been for you—"

"It would've been someone else. And it wasn't only me."

"Yeah, sure, you had a Chinese laundry man, a fat-head army officer, his whelp of a daughter, and a stove-up ol' fart!" Quinby lumbered slowly toward her, his revolver leveled directly at her gut. But that was all right; Jessie had her pistol trained on *his* gut, which was bigger. "Listen—that deal I made you, about the thousand in gold if'n you'd help me; I'll still pay it if you—"

"No, I don't want to listen to any more lies," Jessie said, quoting the sheriff back to him. "You'll get your chance to speak in court."

Quinby fired with the speed of a striking rattler. But Jessie had been watching for those telltale signs in the eyes, in the mannerisms, and caught his mirrored reflex even before his finger completed its move. She sprang aside, his bullet grazing her jacket sleeve. Her pistol spoke once, and more to the point. Quinby twisted, his second shot blowing a hole in his own boot. Jessie fired again as well, catching him in the top of his skull as he fell forward, unable to balance on his remaining foot. He dropped, lifeless.

Meanwhile, Ki kept mercilessly goading his horse faster.

The rasty mustanger seemed to thrive on masochism, fairly burning the rocks as it raced in pursuit. Slowly Ki gained, but Pascal was considerably ahead and managed to reach the mine tunnel before Ki could reach him.

From the soft black of night, they plunged into the almost palpable black of the long tunnel. Ki tried to guide himself by the echo of Pascal's galloping horse, but that didn't work too well. The reverberations swelled to a muddled cacophony. Anyway, by then he'd lost control of his horse. Perversely aroused by plunging hellbent blind down a hole in the ground, the mustanger was stirred to yet greater speed, refusing to obey or come to its senses. Ki was angered—scared, too—feeling that to lose control meant to lose face and quite probably everything else. Still, he was catching up quicker with Pascal, who'd yet to take a spill or miss a beat, and that was worth letting the horse run amok.

They blasted from the tunnel like cannon shells, Ki only a length behind. The gap remained as they rampaged down the cow trail, but they hit the ford and the mustanger proved to be a born swimmer, pulling Ki neck-to-tail with Pascal. Pascal twisted and saw Ki breathing down his back. He spurred his horse to circle, whipped up his revolvers and, snarling curses, squeezed the triggers.

Anticipating the draw, Ki had sprung to balance standing on his horse, then leaped across when Pascal steadied to shoot. Bracketed by flying lead, Ki dove against Pascal, snatched and held one gun-wrist while ripping him off his horse into the river. Still wrapped in a clench, they went down together.

When Pascal plunged into the water, caught by his left wrist, he let go of his revolver and went under, reaching for Ki's throat. He missed that, but he got a stranglehold on Ki's neck for a moment, before Ki broke the hold and twisted the other revolver loose from Pascal's grip. They surfaced struggling. Pascal was a keen, supple fighter—savage and resourceful; but like his type, he was a complex of vicious hates. Ki, wherever he fought, kept a sharp, cool courage, wasting no energy in wild, red fury.

The frigid, roiling water swirled round them as they twisted and turned, attempting to gain a hold, to thrust in, to drag down—anything that might win. They vanished beneath the surface once more. Water began roiling there, and under that muddy veil, they were writhing, fighting in the deep water. Pascal had automatically shut his eyes against the mud. Ki had been trained to keep them open, and to react with lightning speed when he saw an advantage. He kicked at Pascal's inner thigh with his right foot, grabbed a sleeve with his left arm and rammed his palm against the left side of the throat. Pascal rolled over like a baby.

Following, Ki shoved his knees into Pascal's belly. His hands caught hold of the shirt and crossed in the *nami juji jime*, so that his wrists were pressing into Pascal's throat to cut the flow of blood to the brain. Pascal made gurgling, gasping sounds, and clawed, struggling to clutch Ki's wrists. But Ki put his weight behind his crossed forearms, and clamped Pascal down while he rose for a breath of air. Pascal flailed desperately, the terror of death distorting his face.

Ki pushed down harder.

The mud came up into Pascal's open mouth. He started choking, making a gurgling sound low inside his throat, flopping wildly while Ki forced him into the river-bottom mud. His head went deeper, only his quivering nostrils showing. Then they too disappeared. The silty ooze bubbled a couple of times and was still. Ki released his hold on the dead man.

Surfacing, he scanned for the horses. Pascal's mount had the wits to wade ashore, and on the right bank to boot. The mustanger was nowhere to be seen, but somehow, Ki had a hunch Puheska would not be heartbroken. He headed for dry ground and slowly walked, dripping water, to collect the other horse.

Chapter 14

Just before the field by the cabin, Ki came upon Lance Puheska, who was surveying the hills for signs of skirmishes. Dismounting, he ignored Puheska's quizzical look at the horse, giving him the bridle rope with a simple "Thanks."

"Glad to. You return better than you borrow." Leading the horse then, and for reasons of his own, he walked with Ki toward the cabin.

Nearer there, where the carnage was greatest, Jessie, Mulhollan, the major, and Adele were about checking the bodies and securing their prisoners. They were fearful to behold—blackened by gunpowder soot, eyes enflamed from fumes, and smeared with dirt and blood from the heat of action. But they would have been hard pressed to match the fierce Shoshone. If the Indians were savage and courageous on attack, they were absolute terrors in defending their own. A massacre wasn't wise, so reluctantly they took prisoners. But the outlaws were reluctant to be taken prisoner, aware of the hang-noose fate awaiting them. The pitifully few gunmen that remained were bottled up in the rocks, fighting stubbornly. The Shoshone braves didn't need any help, only a little time; let them have the deserved victory.

As Ki and Puheska approached, the others drew to meet them, sounding pleased, relieved, and curious, all together.

"We feared you'd never get here, that you'd both met foul play," Jessie said.

"Sorry, Jess, I went for a river swim to clean off the dirt. Pascal swam too, but he's a poor diver. Forgets to come up." Ki left it at that, shifting attention by saying, "I'm here thanks to Lance. Fact is, he deserves full credit for all of us being here. He sure got here in the nick of time."

"It's the basic rule of cavalry," Puheska allowed dryly.

Mulhollan grinned. "I can't get over your skins savin' our skins."

"You clod," Thinnes snapped. "The Shoshones have been 'friendlies' for years, and've joined with our army against the Sioux and Cheyenne. Why, Chief Washakie, our fort's namesake, an' his warriors fought with Crook at Rosebud."

"And saved the general's skin more'n once," Puheska added. "But look, we didn't know you were here. I went getting some guys I know together, and we chewed over what I'd learned and what we'd do. Sorry, Major. We couldn't trust the army, and we'd lost plenty of stock for a long time, so we figured we'd raid the mine, wreck the loco and stuff, put the Injun-sign fear into 'em. And fast, before you and Ki, Jessie, stirred it sky-high. Our faces pure sank when we found the mine empty, but we figured the loco can't stray far, so we rode huntin' downtrack. Heard the commotion by my place, and . . ." Puheska shrugged, gazing about. "My place's a shambles. Pascal sure made a lot of trouble, sure went to a lot of trouble, but mostly he caused trouble for himself and his gang."

"Pascal wasn't boss," Jessie stated, "he was foreman level. And Ki, no one thought he'd leader skills. The best in prison couldn't boss so complex a plot as was plied here. And how'd Pascal know of it? The boss's here, saw the branding opportunity, and needed rustlers to pull it. He brings in Pascal's cohorts and from that begins the smuggling ring. Pascal gets out, gets on at the LXD, and now the big haul can be made, while acting as front man for the boss. The boss is safer, has his own rackets to play, and offers protection. Until tonight, and if you'll recall, who was shouting orders with Pascal?"

"Sheriff Quinby!" Major Thinnes barked. "And that hellion fooled everybody!" he marveled.

"No reason he shouldn't," Mulhollan returned. "The setup was sweet, and I know enough about cattle to tell yuh their trouble and confusion were worth it. The railroads ended the big long-distance cattle drives, y'see, and ending the drive ended one-shot mass rustlings. Rustlers have to prey directly on ranches now—sneak-thievin', cutting no more than a dozen or so heads at a swipe. Pascal, or Quinby, had *two* one-shot mass rustlings, and the profits from such rustlings would tidily pay for a fancy plan to grab 'em."

"They also needed to rig a scapegoat," Ki went on. "The trouble spent to misdirect the law paid off handsomely, for once on the right track, the crime was easy to solve."

"Well, I'll get my engineers to clean up the train and finish hauling your beef to the fort, Hep," Thinnes remarked. "I reckon this blows the I.G.'s case against you to smithereens."

Jessie gestured off northward. "The simplest thing to do, Major, would be to dispatch some cavalry to catch the original herd Box M sold you. It wears the LXD brand, but that won't make any difference to whoever eats the beef. But it would complicate Hep's efforts to market Box M stuff later on . . ."

. . . And, later on, Jessie had a couple of minutes alone with Lance Puheska; just enough time to say goodbye and make a few brief observations.

"Lance, meeting you has strengthened my hope," she said, running a finger along his cheek. "I believe you did save us accidentally, but I also believe you would've saved us on purpose. Seeing how you and the army cooperate on your reservation convinces me that we can all live in harmony."

"I wish you'd stay longer and see more." Lance smiled with a tired, abiding sadness. "You'd see a reservation is a zoo, run by whites who want the reds off out of the way, and by reds who refuse any change and wish to stay aloof. Well, that's not real; it strains reality, and these reservations will eventually go. The government can't prop them up forever."

"Is that bad, to have the red move out among the white?"

Puheska sighed. "Red and white will eventually go too, the red with his spiritual bond unintelligible in today's terms, and the white with his relentless greed. But perhaps there'll still be time to learn one simple truth—that we are not alone, that man is part of everything that breathes and doesn't, has ever, or will. And we had damn well better watch where we tread."

Watch for

LONE STAR AND THE TONG'S REVENGE

fifty-ninth novel in the exciting
LONE STAR
series from Jove

coming in July!